THE ENTANGLED WEB

LARRY NABBS

Read With You Publishing

Text copyright © 2016 Larry Nabbs

Published by Read With You Publishing

ISBN-13: 978-1-944710-02-6
ISBN-10: 1-944710-02-7

Printed in the United States of America

Contents

CHAPTER 1

Early morning, the narrow street was dark. The black wet surface of the road shone from the previous night's rainfall. A body lying in the road moved. It rolled to the left and into a puddle. The young man groaned, instantly coming awake, and slowly trying to lift himself up. He groaned again at the sharp pain in his side and at the throbbing and painful beating in his head.

"Jesus!" he breathed to himself, forcing himself up onto his knees. His hand touched his head and he felt something sticky, it was blood. He pulled his hand away and looked down at the blood on his fingers.

"What happened?" he asked himself.

Thoughts and images flashed through his mind. There was a blinding light. He squeezed his eyes shut trying to remember and remained still for a few moments, then he opened them again. There was no memory, absolutely none at all about what had happened to him. He looked around and saw that he was sitting in a puddle in a dark narrow street. A blinding light flashed into his mind again and once more he squeezed his eyes tightly shut.

What is it? he thought. The light, what is it? Then the light seemed to fade away and he opened his eyes. He placed his hands down into the puddle, then, groaning with effort, he pushed himself up onto his feet and held onto the body of a nearby parked car to keep his balance. Thunder boomed overhead. He glanced up and saw lightning streak across the dark sky, then he heard more thunder, this time louder than the first. It was going to rain again. Slowly, the man moved his feet forward, letting go of the car and started to stagger along the narrow rain soaked road towards another well-lit street at the far end. A car suddenly turned the corner, its lights blazing as it sped towards him. The man gasped and raised his hands to cover his eyes from the blinding light, then he fell and a swirl-pool of blackness enveloped him once more.

CHAPTER 2

The young man's eyes fluttered open. The light of the room made him blink. Slowly, and with a groan, he pulled himself up onto his elbow. He glanced around the room. It was furnished with a bed, a dresser, a night table and a wardrobe. Sunlight streamed in through the white-laced curtains which covered the open window on the far side of the room billowing inwards from a breeze outside. He looked across at the photo of his ex-girlfriend which he still kept on his dresser. He was in his own bedroom, in his own apartment, but ... how did he get there? The question raced through his mind as he tried to remember.

Suddenly, the bedroom door opened.

"Oh! You're awake!" said a tall and very pretty blonde girl coming into the room and gazing down at him with a look of surprise. The young man stared up at her, then suddenly realized that beneath the covers of the bed he was completely naked. He looked underneath the covers to check and blushed slightly.

"Who ... who are you?" he asked, staring back up at the girl.

The girl came further into the room carrying a pair of pajamas.

"I … I was just going to dress you in these," she said, throwing the pajamas onto the bed. "They're dry. I found them hanging up next to your washing machine."

The young man continued to stare up at her, taking no notice of the pajamas she'd thrown at him.

"I said … who are you?" the young man, repeated with an annoyed tone to his voice.

The girl smiled, moved closer to the bed and sat down on it beside him.

"My name's Julia Jones," she said with a smile. "I almost ran you over. I was going to take you to the hospital, but you kept murmuring 'no hospital, no doctors', so, I found your address in your wallet and brought you home. Your name's Daniel McGlade, you live in a nice apartment overlooking the beach, and you're a private detective, that's what I know about you so far, so, what happened to you?"

Daniel stared at her in silence for a few moments. He tried to think, tried to remember. Images flashed into his mind but the images moved too fast and he couldn't make anything out of them clearly, apart from a white light, a blinding white light.

"I … I don't know," Daniel said.

He put a hand to his head and found a bandage which the girl, Julia Jones, had placed around his head to cover a wound.

"I …I suppose I should thank you," he said.

Julia shrugged, "Well, that's what most people would do. Lucky for you I was a trained nurse before I decided to change my job."

Daniel studied her for a moment. She was very attractive, possibly in her mid-twenties, with short blonde hair and blue eyes. He studied her clothes, she looked like a student with a red check shirt, faded blue jeans and white trainers.

"Well, thanks again," Daniel said. "Now, if you don't mind, I think I'll get up."

"Hey!" Julia said, holding out her hand to stop him. "You're hurt, you need to rest, at least for one day."

Daniel looked at her.

"I'm going to get up," he said firmly. "If you want to see my naked body, which you've obviously already seen, go ahead."

"I … I had to undress you," Julia said, seemingly slightly embarrassed. "Your clothes were soaking wet."

"Right, whatever … now, do you want to have another free show?"

Julia looked down at him for a moment, then stood up and turned to the door.

"It's your funeral!" she said, leaving the bedroom.

The moment the door closed shut behind her, Daniel got up out of bed. He immediately took some clothes out of the wardrobe and dresser and got dressed, then he checked the drawer at the bottom of the dresser and found the spare gun and ammunition that he kept there. He checked the gun to make sure that it was loaded, put the box of extra cartridges in his pocket, then left the bedroom. Julia was standing on the balcony as he entered the living room. After the night's storm, it was a beautiful sunny day. She stood gazing down at the beach and the ocean below. Daniel stepped out onto the balcony through the sliding glass doors to join her.

"Nice view," she said, turning to him as he came up beside her.

"It's okay," Daniel said.

Julia looked at his clothes.

"Do you always wear black?" she asked.

"It's my favourite colour."

She smiled, "I see. I, er ... made a hot coffee for you, it's on the table in the kitchen."

"Thanks."

"You know, you really should rest up, at least for one day."

Daniel shook his head, "Sorry nurse, can't do that, I've got business to attend to."

"I'm not a nurse anymore."

"You're 'my' nurse."

Julia grinned, "Yes, I am, aren't I?" she said.

Daniel glanced down at the ocean four floors below, then looked back at Julia.

"I'd like you to go now," he said.

Julia gazed at him, a surprised look on her face.

"I ... I'd like to stay with you, make sure you're okay."

"Don't you have something else to do?"

"Are you trying to get rid of me?"

"Is it that obvious?"

"You know, I think that bump on your head is more important than I thought."

"Oh really? Why's that?"

"You seem to have lost your social skills."

Daniel smiled, "How do you know I had any in the first place?"

"I don't, but most people do."

"You know, you're right."

"About what?"

"I 'am' trying to get rid of you."

Julia stared at him with an expression of anger on her face.

"Is this how you treat people who help you?"

"You should see how I treat my enemies!"

"Oh, I'm sure you have a lot of those!" Julia said.

She suddenly turned and moved past him to leave the balcony. Daniel followed after her into the living room and watched while Julia picked up her bag and raincoat. Julia walked to the door, opened it, then glanced back.

"Don't forget your coffee," she said. "I hope you choke on it!"

Daniel smiled and watched as she went out and slammed the door shut. He looked around the room to make sure that everything was in place, then glanced at his watch. It was still morning. His mind was a mess. He remained still, thinking, trying to remember what had happened. A sudden jumble of images came to him from nowhere. The only thing that stuck in his mind was a café at the railway station. A café … a table … a phone call … a meeting. The images were all mixed up, turning, spinning, as voices came from nowhere, indistinguishable, men's voices …

Daniel rubbed his eyes, then turned and went into the kitchen. He found the hot cup of coffee where Julia had left it on the table and sat down. His wallet, keys and car keys plus some other things that he usually carried around with him were also on the table. There was also a mobile phone that he didn't recognize. He picked it up looking at it curiously. Only two things were missing, the gun he usually carried, and his own mobile phone. He was at least thankful for the spare gun he always kept in his drawer. He drank the coffee, savouring the taste, then stood up putting all of his things into his pockets including the new mobile phone. Suddenly, he stopped, seeing another flash. The image of a café at the train station came quickly into in his mind with a searing pain, and then it left him as quickly as it had appeared. He gasped, leaning against the chair for a moment, then he turned, left the kitchen, and walked across the living room to the door. Another image of the train station hit him as he reached for the door's handle. He squeezed his eyes shut and put his hand to his head feeling the sharp searing pain turn into a pain that now throbbed in his head as if someone was hitting his head with a hammer from inside. He groaned, standing still for a moment until both the image and the pain had passed, then he sighed from relief, reached forward, opened the door and left his apartment as quickly as possible. As he rode down in the lift, he was hoping that his car would be where he usually left it in the building's underground car park.

It wasn't.

He stood for a long moment in the car park staring at his parking space, wondering where the hell his car was.

CHAPTER 3

Daniel took a bus to the train station, walked through it, passing various station shops, and then found the café on the other side nearby an exit. As he stepped inside gazing around, images flashed into his mind once more.

People.

The café had been crowded.

After a moment, the images left him and he suddenly realized that he was standing in the way of the door hindering people who were trying to move past him to get inside.

"I'm sorry," he said, looking at them and moving aside to let them pass. He remained still after the people passed, looking around at the café in front of him. It was almost empty. The public address system in the station outside announced a train about to leave its platform and go to another city further up along the coast. Daniel glanced at his watch, it was still early, not even lunch time yet. He moved forward and went over to the café's bar and sat down on one of the stools. He glanced around at the few people sitting at the tables who had probably just arrived after taking a train, or were waiting to take a train to go somewhere else. The café's assistant came over to him and placed her hands down on the bar in front of him.

"What can I get you?" she asked.

Daniel looked at her, she was young, with dark shoulder-length hair and a pretty face. Her eyes were partly hidden beneath her hair which hung down over them. If she hadn't been working in the café he would have taken her for a punk. He glanced at the name on her badge.

"Heather, right?"

Heather smiled, "Right," she said. "You get ten points for being able to read. Now, what can I get you?"

Daniel grinned, "Do you remember if I was in here before?"

"What? You can't remember?"

"If I could remember I wouldn't be asking."

Heather looked at the bandage on Daniel's head.

She nodded, "Right. Yeah, I remember you."

"Oh, really? Weren't there a lot of people here?"

"Sure there were, but I always remember someone who breaks one of our cups."

"Oops, sorry."

Heather grinned, "Don't worry, you paid for it. You and the other man were arguing."

"The other man?"

"A big guy, older than you. You suddenly stood up from the table and the cup fell onto the floor."

"Did you hear what we were arguing about?"

Heather shook her head, "There were too many people here, it was noisy. What happened to your head?"

"I had an accident."

She stared at him for a moment studying the bandage on his head and the bruise on his face.

"Yeah, looks like it," she said. "You okay?"

Daniel nodded, "Was there anything else?" he asked.

"Maybe."

"Maybe what?"

"Well, that depends, if you've come in here to ask questions or if you're actually going to order something."

Daniel smiled to himself thinking you never get something for nothing.

He shrugged, "Okay. What did I have last time?"

"Café latte."

"Good memory."

Heather smiled, "For some things," she said.

"I'll have the same," Daniel said. He leaned forward onto the bar, "Now … can you remember anything else?"

"Yeah, there was something else. You both left. Apparently you went to get a taxi, but there were too many people waiting for taxis, so you came back to order one."

"A taxi?" Daniel repeated. He gazed down trying desperately to remember. "What time was it?"

"About 1 o'clock yesterday afternoon."

"Do you remember the taxi company?"

"Sure, we always use the same one, unless they're all busy of course."

Heather walked over to the cash register, picked up a card, then came back and handed it to him.

"That's the company," she said.

"Thanks," Daniel said, reading the taxi company's name, address and phone number.

"Now, if you don't mind," Heather said, observing him with a smile, "I'll go prepare your café latte."

Daniel watched her walk away, then pulled out his new mobile phone and dialed the taxi company's number.

"Yeah … hello?" Daniel said into the phone.

"Hello?" came a man's gruff voice.

"Is this the 'Go To Anywhere Taxi company'?"

"How do you know about us?"

"I have your card."

"And what does it say on the card?"

"The Go To Anywhere Taxi Company."

"Then, yeah, I guess that's who we are. Thanks for reminding me!"

Daniel rolled his eyes.

"Where are you and where do you want to go?" the man asked. "And please don't say Tokyo, we may be called 'Go to Anywhere' but we 'do' have our limits!"

"I'm at a train station and I just want some information about a pick up outside The Carriage Café yesterday around 1pm."

"Don't you want to go anywhere?"

"Not sure yet, maybe."

"Maybe? Look, we're a taxi company, not an information service."

Daniel didn't like the man's tone, he gripped the phone tightly.

"Okay, send me a taxi, but make it the same driver who came yesterday afternoon."

"Well, that could take a little longer."

"I'll wait."

Daniel turned off the phone and put the new mobile back into his pocket.

"Here's your coffee," Heather said, placing his café latte down onto the bar in front of him.

"Thanks," Daniel said.

Heather leaned forward onto the bar as he reached to pick up the cup.

"I have one question," she said.

Daniel looked at her.

"Okay," he said.

Heather bit her lip, hesitating as if she was afraid to ask.

"I … I get off at 6pm, will you be around?"

Daniel grinned back at her, "I don't know," he said.

Heather nodded, a look of disappointment on her face, "Okay then, … enjoy your coffee."

"Thanks," Daniel said, then turned away and carried his coffee over to a table nearby the window looking out onto the street. As he sat drinking his coffee, Daniel gazed out of the window at the people passing by and those trying to get a taxi outside the station. It seemed that taxis were in demand, there was already a long queue of people waiting at the taxi stand. He observed the people standing there waiting. An image flashed ran through his mind again. Daniel closed his eyes trying to remember. A light … a bright light! Pain! Pain! He almost cried out, then opened his eyes quickly, stopping himself before he did. Heather, standing behind the bar, was observing him strangely. Daniel ventured a half smile towards her. She smiled back at him, then turned away to serve another customer. Daniel sat studying her for a moment. He found her attractive. He liked the way that her dark hair hung down over her eyes, almost hiding them and giving her a shaggy look. Maybe the punk look was back in fashion, he thought. He studied her for a few moments more, in two minds whether or not he should take up her offer, then he turned and once again looked out of the window. After a few minutes, he noticed a man wearing a brown jacket and beige trousers standing nearby the taxi stand. He must have been in his forties, neat haircut, well-shaved. Every once in a while he would glance towards the café. Daniel began to have the uneasy feeling that he was being watched. Little by little, the man moved along the taxi queue to the front. When it came to his turn and a taxi pulled up beside him he stepped back, allowing the woman behind him to go in front. The woman was very thankful, but as she was thanking him, the man glanced over to the café where Daniel was sitting. Daniel was now certain that this man, whoever he was, was watching him. Daniel took out his mobile phone, pressed the button for camera mode, and then quickly took a photo of the man now standing next to the taxi stand but out of the queue. Daniel studied the image he had captured on his mobile and blew up the face. He had never seen the man before, at least, as far as he knew, considering that he couldn't remember any recent events. He looked back up, but this time the man was gone. Suddenly, he felt someone standing beside him. Daniel turned and saw a younger man wearing a light coloured short-sleeved shirt.

"The girl at the bar tells me you're the one who ordered the taxi," the man said.

"Er … yes, yes, I did. Please … sit down."

The taxi driver studied him, "You mean, you don't want to go anywhere? I have my taxi right outside," he said, pointing towards the street.

"Just sit down for a minute," Daniel said, gesturing towards the empty seat opposite him.

The taxi driver shrugged, "Okay,"

he said, and sat down.

"Heather … er … the girl behind the bar, tells me you picked me up from this cafe yesterday afternoon around 1 o'clock."

The man studied Daniel carefully, then pointed a finger at his face, "Yeah, that's right. You're the guy who didn't know where he was going, the other guy did."

"And … where did you take us?"

The taxi driver looked at the bandage on Daniel's head.

"What's the matter? You can't remember things?" he asked.

Daniel sighed, tired of hearing the same question.

"Yes, that's right. Now … where did you take us?"

"Out in the suburbs to the west," the taxi driver said. "The other guy made me stop in a quiet road, no houses, just warehouses."

"Did we go into a warehouse?"

The taxi driver stared at him.

"Normally, it's not my business where my fares go once they get out of my taxi," he said.

Daniel leaned forward, "But …?"

The taxi driver shrugged again.

"Well, this was a little different. I mean, I drop the two of you off in the middle of nowhere where there are only a few empty and abandoned warehouses … I was a little curious."

"So … you saw which building we went into?"

The taxi driver hesitated for a moment, then shrugged again, "Yeah, you went into the red-brick warehouse."

Daniel stared thoughtfully down at his coffee. He tried to remember, but no image of a red-brick warehouse came into his mind.

Suddenly, he stood up.

"Take me there," he said.

The taxi driver looked up at him.

"Are you sure? It's a little far."

Daniel nodded, "Take me there," he said again.

CHAPTER 4

As the taxi weaved through the city's traffic towards the suburbs in the west, Daniel sat on the back seat thinking. Why would he take a taxi when he had a car? he wondered. And where the hell was his car? His thoughts were interrupted by the ringing tone of his new mobile phone. He took it out of his pocket, looked at it with an expression of surprise, then answered it.

"Yes?" he said.

"Hi! How are you feeling?" a girl's voice asked.

"Let me guess, this is nursie," Daniel said.

"Er … just Julia is okay."

"Let me guess, you saw I had lost my mobile phone so you bought me a new one, right?"

"Er … I was just trying to help."

"Nice of you. Thanks,"

"Wow! You can be nice after all!"

"Tell me, when you undressed me, did you take photos of me naked and show them to all your friends?"

Julia laughed, "Ha, ha, ha. I'm not that kind of girl!"

"Okay Julia, so, what are you doing? Are you stalking me?"

Julia laughed again, "Now, why would I do that?"

"Search me," Daniel said. "Some girls have very strange ideas."

"Some guys too."

"Yeah, right, but don't digress. What do you want?"

There was a silence on the other end of the line.

"You really should improve your manners," Julia said. "Okay, I'm phoning to find out how you are, although considering your attitude I don't know why, and I'm also phoning about your car. Due to your memory problem, I thought you might like to know where you left it, just in case you forgot that too."

Daniel remained silent with the phone to his ear for a moment.

"My car?" he said finally. "How do you know about my car? How do you know where I left it?"

I saw a photo of you in your apartment standing next to your girlfriend nearby an old yellow Volkswagen Beetle, I noticed the license plate."

Once again, Daniel remained quiet for a moment before answering.

"My ex-wife," he said, almost vacantly.

"Oh, sorry, your 'ex'-wife. I can understand that. Anyway, I know where your car is, in case you don't remember."

"Where?" Daniel asked.

"It's in the same street where I almost ran you down."

"And … which street is that?"

There was a pause.

"Wow! You really don't remember anything, do you?"

"I only have a problem remembering recent things," Daniel said. "I remember who I am at least."

"So, not a total loss right?" Julia said.

"Where's my car Julia?" Daniel said, growing impatient. "Which street is it in?"

He heard Julia sigh into the phone, "It's in Turner street, in the night-club district," she said after a moment.

"Turner street?" Daniel said to himself, trying to remember.

"That's right. No need to thank me, although, a dinner might be nice."

"A dinner?" Daniel repeated. "I'll think about it."

"Daniel McGlade, you really need to work on your charms, you know?"

The taxi driver turned glancing back at him.

"Almost there," he said. "The warehouses are just around the bend."

Daniel nodded and spoke again into the phone.

"I've got to go!" he said

"Daniel …!" he heard Julia say, just before he turned off the phone.

The taxi turned around a bend and a row of deserted looking warehouses came into sight. The taxi drove past the first few buildings and then came to a stop nearby a large red-brick warehouse. The building looked as if it had been deserted for years.

The taxi driver turned again.

"Do you want me to wait for you?" he asked.

Daniel sat looking at the warehouse, then shook his head, "No." he said. "I might be a while."

The taxi driver shrugged, "Suit yourself," he said.

Daniel paid the fare, then got out of the taxi and watched it leave before turning towards the warehouse. The building rose up before him. Once a place of buzzing activity, it now stood completely silent like a monster laid to rest. Daniel took out the gun from his holster, checked to see if he had a bullet in the chamber, took of the safety catch, then began walking towards the building's large green doors. As he neared the doors he saw that one of them was slightly open. He raised his gun, aiming it in front of him, then stepped inside. Various objects littered the warehouse floor. Daniel walked across the warehouse slowly, looking around and keeping his gun ready. He stopped almost in its centre. There seemed to be nothing strange about the place, it looked merely like any other abandoned warehouse. He noticed a door on the far side in front of him. He paused, staring across at it, then slowly walked towards it through the debris littering the deserted warehouse floor. When he reached the door, he listened for a moment but heard nothing. He tried the door's handle and found that it was unlocked. He pushed the door forward slowly, hearing it creak in the surrounding silence. When the door was fully open, he saw a staircase leading down. He searched the wall for a light-switch, found it and turned it on. As the light came on, he was surprised to see that the electricity still worked. He hesitated, listening, then moved forward and began walking down the steps. Half-way down, the staircase twisted to the left. He followed the way round descending the steps and a few moments later he found himself in a large basement with a corridors leading off in three different directions. A faint sound seemed to be coming from the central corridor. He stared towards it, then moved across the basement floor and entered the corridor. As he walked along the corridor looking both left and right, he saw empty rooms with nothing inside except old dusty tables, chairs and various pieces of furniture. The sound he had heard was a humming sound. It was coming from one of the rooms half-way along the corridor on the right. Daniel slowed his steps and moved towards it carefully, keeping his gun aimed forward at hip level ready to fire. As he neared the room, he saw that a faint blue light was coming from inside. Daniel stopped as he reached the open doorway, then carefully looked inside. What he saw made his eyes widen in shock.

CHAPTER 5

Daniel stepped inside the dimly-lit room staring down at the body of an older man. He had apparently been neatly dressed, but his trousers and underpants had been pulled down exposing his body, naked from below his waist. His hair was black but graying at the sides giving him a distinguished look. He stared up at Daniel with lifeless unseeing eyes, his mouth open as if he were about to scream. His wrists were bound to two metal rings set into the wall behind him. His legs were bound widely apart with rope around his ankles attached to two other metal rings in the wall near the floor. His semi-clothed, semi-naked body had wires attached to it. The wires, which were attached to certain sensitive parts of his body, as well as in other places, continued to give his body electric shocks even though he was now dead. The other end of the wires were attached to a machine set on a wooden table in front of him. Near the table were two empty wooden chairs which were facing him as if someone had been sitting there watching the man's tortured agony from the electricity coursing through his body. The faint blue light was coming from the electrical wires which continued to travel from the machine on the table and along the wires attached to him. Daniel found the light-switch and turned on the light. The man's body was twisted in its bonds as if he was trying to free himself from his agony. The scene of torture and death in front of Daniel looked grotesque, as if it were an image from a horror movie. Daniel stepped forward and turned off the machine. The blue light from the electricity running along the wires stopped as did the humming sound. Daniel remained still for a moment, staring at the dead man as if he were in a state of shock. Finally, he moved forward over to the man and started going through his pockets. He found the man's wallet and opened it. Inside, there was a company pass card with his name, office address and number, as well as other business cards. There was some cash, a credit card and some personal cards with his home address. His name was John Keaton and according to his business card, he was in the insurance business. Whoever killed him didn't need this information. Possibly they were after something else, something that he knew, but what? Daniel took the company pass card and one of his personal cards and put the wallet back in the dead man's inside pocket, then he stepped back, staring at the man's half naked body and the various wires attached to him. Was this the man he had met at the café? he thought. He glanced down at the man's photo on the company pass card. The man's smiling face in the photo didn't jog anything in Daniel's memory. He looked at the man again, at his wide staring eyes and his grotesque expression which made it seem as if he were still screaming, but with a silent scream of death. No one deserves to die like this, Daniel thought to himself, no one. He sighed sadly, staring at the man, then put the cards in his pocket and turned to leave. Suddenly, he heard a noise from somewhere above him. Someone else was in the warehouse. Daniel remained still, listening, then once again raised his gun. He moved as quietly as he could back across the room and paused at the open doorway looking out into the corridor outside. The corridor was empty. He stepped out into it and began moving slowly along the corridor back the way he had come listening carefully. When he reached the steps going up, he hesitated. He gripped his gun tightly in his hand, then slowly began to mount the steps up towards the door above. As he was almost halfway up, he heard the noise again. He stopped, his heart pounding as he listened carefully. He waited for a moment, heard nothing more, then continued on up the steps. When he reached the door at the top, he stopped. He paused, looking at the door in front of him, then reached forward and slowly opened it. The door creaked open in the silence and Daniel gritted his teeth as he held his gun ready to fire. From the view that he had of the large warehouse floor, the warehouse seemed empty. He stepped through the open doorway slowly, looking around as he went. Suddenly, a man appeared from behind one of the warehouse's columns. Daniel immediately recognized him. He was the man who had been standing in the taxi queue outside the station café.

Daniel raised his gun, aiming it carefully at the man as the man began to grin at him.

"Hey!" Daniel called out. "Who are you?"

The man merely stared back at him in silence and continued to grin. Daniel remained still, staring at the man, confused as to why the man was grinning, then he heard a noise behind him, but it was too late, as something hit him on the back of the head. A blackness engulfed him and images swirled around in his head as he seemed to be falling, falling into some deep dark hole.

CHAPTER 6

"Where is she?"

The man's voice seemed to come to Daniel through a thick fog. The voice sounded distorted, as if it were coming through a tunnel from far away, as if it were part of a long forgotten dream. The punch to his face was like an explosion to his brain with bright sparks of light followed by pain. Slowly, Daniel opened his eyes. As he eyes began to focus, he saw that he was in a small dimly-lit room which seemed bare of furniture, save for a few wooden chairs and a wooden table. The man standing in front of him and staring down at him was big, very big and muscular, and his face was scarred and had a broken nose as if he had been a boxer. Daniel tried to move and found that he'd been tied to a chair. The man spoke down to him again, louder this time.

"I said, where is she?"

Daniel stared up at him, then noticed two other men standing behind him. Daniel recognized the man on the left as the man in the warehouse who had grinned at him.

"You want some more?" the big man standing in front of him asked with a sneer on his face. The man's fist came crashing down again making contact with Daniels face and jerking his head to the right with the force of the blow.

"Now, where is she?" the big man asked again.

Daniel felt blood running down from his cut lit as he looked back up at the big man.

"You want to stop tickling me and tell me who the hell 'she' is?" Daniel managed to say.

The big man leaned down towards him, "Don't play games with us! We know you know who 'she' is!"

Daniel shook his head, "Don't know what you're talking about," he said. "Don't know who 'she' is, don't know who 'you' are … hell! I barely know who 'I' am!"

The big man punched him again and Daniel cried out from the pain. His head slumped forward and blood now ran down from his lips and onto his chest staining his shirt.

"This is getting us nowhere!" said the man who'd been standing in the taxi queue. He took out a knife, "Let me have a go at him!"

The big man looked at the knife in the other man's hand and grinned, "Okay,' he said. "You take over. I need a rest anyway."

Both the big man and the third man, who seemed to be smartly dressed in a dark suit, turned and left the room. The man with the knife came over and looked down at Daniel.

"You think you're a tough guy?" he asked. He grinned, "You know, people say I'm really good with a knife. Let me show you how good I am!"

Daniel noticed the scar on the side of the man's face.

"Oh, really? So, where'd you get the scar?" he asked. "Did you cut yourself shaving?"

The man's grin faded as he continued looking at him, "Yeah, how'd you guess? You're a funny guy, right? Well, let's see if you find what happens next is so funny!"

He reached forward to Daniel with the knife.

"Now," the man said, once again grinning as he spoke, "if this doesn't make you talk, nothing will."

Daniel pulled at the bonds holding him firmly in the chair.

"Don't bother," the man said, watching Daniel trying to free himself. "I tie pretty good knots. Tell me when you're ready to talk!"

"I don't know anything!" Daniel shouted, staring at him "I don't remember anything!"

The man paused, staring into Daniel's eyes as he pressed the knife against him

"Well, we'll soon find out, won't we?" he said.

Daniel squeezed his eyes shut, clenching his teeth tightly together as he tensed, pulling helplessly at the bonds binding him to the chair.

Suddenly, a voice spoke from behind the man.

"Untie him!" said the voice.

The man crouching down in front of Daniel hesitated, holding the knife tightly in his hand. He seemed to be thinking, judging the distance behind him and the time it would take to turn and throw the knife. From the sound of the voice, he knew that it was a girl standing behind him, but did she have a gun aimed at him? The man licked his lips nervously, if she had a gun, he thought, he'd be dead before he could even make the turn.

"I said untie him!" the girl's voice said again.

Daniel, still sitting tensely in his bonds, slowly opened his eyes and stared past the man and up at the girl. He gasped in surprise, recognizing her as the blonde girl who had helped him called Julia. The man licked his lips nervously again, then decided against trying anything. He took the knife away from Daniel then reached forward and began cutting through the rope binding Daniel to the chair. The moment that Daniel was freed from the chair he quickly stood and pulled his trousers back up.

"Drop the knife!" Julia said from behind the man.

The man dropped the knife, letting it clatter to the floor noisily.

"Stand up and turn around!" Julia ordered.

The man complied, and as he did so he saw the gun in Julia's hand she had aimed towards him.

Julia glanced at Daniel, "Are you okay?" she asked.

Daniel nodded, gazing at her and rubbing the soreness out of his wrists. He bent down, picked up the knife and stepped over to the man.

"You know, I'm pretty good with a knife myself," he said, staring bitterly into the man's eyes. Daniel threw him a punch before the man could do or say anything and then watched as the man collapsed down onto the floor unconscious.

"Come on!" Julia said, behind him. "We've got to go! The others may be back soon!"

Daniel turned to look at her, then nodded, "I've got a lot of questions to ask you!" he said, moving over to her.

Julia nodded back to him, "Okay! But when we're out of here! Let's go!"

Daniel followed her out into the corridor and saw that he was once again down in the basement. Julia ran along the corridor with Daniel behind her and they reached the steps leading up. They both ran up the steps two at a time and when they burst out of the door at the top Julia had her gun ready in front of her to ready to shoot. A shout came from the other side of the warehouse and a gun was fired. Both Julia and Daniel ducked as Julia fired back and ran across the warehouse to the right followed by Daniel. Daniel glanced to the left as he ran and saw both the big man and the man in the smart dark suit chasing them.

The big man was the one who was holding a gun and firing at them. A bullet passed close by hitting the wall behind Daniel. He heard Julia shout something from in front and ran as fast as he could behind her as she made her way towards the warehouse exit. Another bullet ricocheted off the wall beside Daniel as he ran, and then both Julia and he were going through the open door of the warehouse and

running outside.

"This way!" Julia shouted back, leading him across the road towards a parked car. Julia opened the door of the car and jumped in behind the steering wheel as Daniel ran around and quickly got in on the other side. Julia started the car's engine just as the two men exited from the warehouse and the big man raised his gun and fired at them. Julia quickly put the car in gear and jerked the car forward, its tyres screeching on the road as it started to speed away from the warehouse leaving the two men in the road behind to stare after them.

CHAPTER 7

Daniel opened his eyes.

Julia was standing in front of him offering him a cup with something hot to drink inside.

"How do you feel?" she asked.

Daniel sat up in the armchair and took the cup from her.

"Headache," Daniel said. "Like I've been hit by a truck."

Julia sat down on the sofa opposite and smiled across at him, "That's not surprising. The guy who beat you looked like he used to be a professional boxer."

Daniel took a sip of the hot drink. It was coffee. He looked around the room, "So, this is your place?" he asked.

Julia nodded, "It's not much, but it's home. Anyway, it's better than going to your place for the moment, they might know where you live."

Daniel studied the room. Julia was being modest, the living room was large and nicely furnished.

"Nice place," Daniel said.

"Thanks."

He looked at her, studying her carefully.

"So,' he said finally. "Just who the hell are you? And don't tell me you're a nurse."

Julia gazed back at him with a smile, "Well, you could thank first," she said. "You know, for saving your life, a second time!"

"Thanks," Daniel said, staring at her curiously. "Now, who the hell are you?"

"Well, I can see you haven't changed," Julia said. "That fresh hit on the head hasn't helped to make you one bit more hospitable."

"It's my character," Daniel said. "Learn to live with it. Now, for the last time, who the hell are you?"

Julia sighed, then shrugged her shoulders, "okay," she said. "Let's just say that I'm one of the good guys, and I'm the girl trying to save your ass."

Daniel stared at her for a moment, then shook his head, "That doesn't tell me anything," he said.

Julia leaned towards him, a smile once again on her face, "You still don't remember anything, do you?"

Daniel stared at her, then glanced down at the cup of coffee in his hand and shook his head.

"No, I … I still don't remember," he said.

"Well, maybe you're lucky I came along when I did, that guy with the knife looked like he meant business!"

Daniel closed his eyes remembering the knife being pressed against him, "Yeah … thanks again for that," he said.

"Now, this time, I really want you to have a rest for one day."

"But …"

"Hey, I'm being kind! Normally, you should at least rest over for one week!"

She raised a small mirror up in front of him and Daniel saw his face. It was badly bruised.

"Rub this onto your face," Julia said, now holding up a tube of medical cream.

Daniel took the tube and stared down at it.

"I'll leave this for you too," Julia said, placing a gun down onto the small coffee table, "just in case! You never know, right?"

Daniel glanced down at the gun, "Loaded?" he asked.

"Of course!" Julia said.

She stood up, "I'm going to go now. I'll bring you back some clean clothes. If you're hungry, there's some food I left for you in the kitchen."

Daniel looked up at her.

"Julia ... who are you really?"

Julia looked back down at him.

"You get some rest," she said, turning towards the door.

"Er ... Julia? Abut the clothes ..."

"I know," Julia said back to him as she reached the door, "The clothes must be black, you always wear black. It matches your black character, right?"

Daniel shrugged, "Call it a habit," he said.

Julia smiled, "Black it is!" then she left and closed the door behind her.

Daniel stared towards the closed door, then took another sip of his coffee and stood up. He walked across the room to the window and looked out. The night was black, but the sky was cloudless and clear with twinkling stars and a half-moon. He noticed that Julia's apartment was high up and, like his, not far from the ocean. Far away, on the horizon, he could see the distant lights of a ship. He stared at it for a moment, wondering where it had come from and where it was going, then he glanced down at the street below. The dark street looked wet, as if it had been raining again. He saw Julia exit the building. She walked across the street to her car and got in. As she turned on the engine and the lights and then drove away, another car's headlights came on a few cars behind from where she'd been parked and pulled away from the kerb to follow her. Daniel stared down at the car as it followed Julia's along the street, then quickly pulled out his mobile phone and dialed Julia's number. The line rang but there was no answer.

"Come on!" Daniel whispered to himself. "Pick up! Pick up!"

Suddenly, he heard a noise at the door. Daniel quickly turned and went back across the room. He saw the gun which Julia had left for him on the coffee table and picked it up. He checked to make sure that Julia was telling the truth and that it was loaded, it was. Daniel gripped the gun tightly in his hand, then went over to the door. Someone was placing a key, or something, into the lock. The lock 'clicked', and then the handle of the door slowly turned. Daniel held his breath as he aimed the gun towards the door with both hands. He stood quietly, ready to fire at whoever came through the door.

CHAPTER 8

The large office was in semi darkness. At least twelve people sat on both sides of the long

board -room styled table. The man at the end, who appeared to be in his sixties, placed his hands onto the edge of the long table.

"Give me your reports," he said, in a deep anxious-filled voice.

A woman with dark hair, two people down from his right, leaned forward.

"We have a problem," she said.

Everyone looked at her.

"Go on," said the man sitting at the head of the table.

"The prime subject, agent 24, is missing, and, I believe, has either been captured or killed. Also, another element has entered the picture."

"Another element?" the man at the head of the table said.

"Yes," the woman replied. "A young man named Daniel McGlade."

"What do we know about him?" the man sitting on the woman's left asked.

The woman flipped a switch on the remote control which had been lying on the table in front of her. A large image appeared on a screen on the wall to the right. The image was a photograph of a young man in his twenties, possibly late twenties. His face looked youthful, but there was something hard in his stare. He was medium height, medium build with jet black hair.

"This is Daniel McGlade," the woman said. "He grew up in an orphanage, hence, no family. He ran away from the orphanage, then came to the city and practiced boxing. He got quite good at it and became a boxer at a young age under the nickname 'The Black Cat'. Later, he joined the police. There was a bribe scandal. There was no conclusive proof that he took bribes, however, the suspicion of the scandal stuck to him making him leave the police. He became a private detective. He's known for being stubborn and getting to the bottom of things. He's divorced, no children and he lives alone on Seaview Boulevard."

"A nice address," said a man at the other end of the table. "Maybe there was something to the bribe story."

"How is he connected?" the man sitting at the end of the table asked.

"We believe he was the last person to see agent 24 before he disappeared," the woman answered.

The man at the end of the table gazed thoughtfully down at his entwined fingers.

"I see," he said finally. "Then, we must find him, and find out what he knows, then … he must be eliminated."

The woman nodded, "I'll see to it," she said.

*

Daniel stood with his feet apart and his two hands on the gun, aiming it towards the door.

Suddenly, there was a loud crashing noise.

Daniel jerked towards the sound to his left. There was shouting next door. A man and a woman were shouting and having an argument. Daniel turned his attention back to the door, gripping the gun tightly in his hands. The handle of the door had stopped turning. Daniel waited, then after a moment, slowly moved towards it. He kept the gun held tightly in his right hand and reached out towards the door-handle with his left. He grasped the door-handle, then quickly turned it and swung the door open, aiming his gun straight ahead.

There was nobody there.

Slowly, Daniel moved forward and looked out into the corridor. The corridor was completely empty. Daniel breathed a sigh of relief, suddenly realizing that he'd been holding his breath. He looked both left and right along the corridor for a few moments, murmuring something under his breath, then he turned back into the apartment and closed the door. He glanced down at his right hand, it was still gripping the gun tightly. Daniel breathed another sigh of relief, then looked around the room. He checked the drawers of a nearby desk, then went into the bedroom and bathroom searching for anything that could shed a light on who Julia Jones really was.

Who was she? What was she not telling him? And just who was the dead man at the warehouse? Daniel had his name and occupation, but it didn't really tell him just 'who' he really was. What was it the men at the warehouse wanted to know? Daniel thought to himself. Where is she? they had asked him. Where is who? he thought. Were they looking for Julia? Someone else? Where is who? This was the question that was now burning inside him, where is who? Whoever it was, she was the key to this whole business, Daniel thought.

Finding nothing of interest in the apartment, not even a photograph, Daniel sat back down in an armchair thinking. After a moment, he glanced back up and gazed carefully around at the living room in front of him. As he looked at the desk, he suddenly noticed that there was something strange about the drawer. He had closed it when he had looked into it earlier, and yet, it didn't seem to be fully closed. Had he not been sitting and staring at it, maybe he wouldn't have noticed. Daniel got up and went over to the desk. He opened the drawer and tried closing it again. Once again, the drawer didn't quite close completely. Daniel crouched down, then pulled the drawer out of the desk and laid it down on the floor beside him, next, he reached forward feeling the back of the desk onto which the drawer would normally close. After a moment, his fingers found a button underneath a small metal covering which moved easily aside. He paused, holding his breath, then pushed the button. There was a 'click' and then beside him, a small secret drawer opened out from the desk. Daniel stood up and opened the drawer more fully towards him looking inside it as he did so.

What he saw made him gasp in surprise.

"What the hell …!" he mouthed to himself.

And then he jerked back up as his mobile phone rang.

CHAPTER 9

Daniel answered the phone, still staring down at the contents inside the secret drawer.

"Yes?" he answered.

At first, there was no sound, not even the sound of someone breathing.

"Hello?" Daniel said again. "Hello? Is anyone there?"

Suddenly, a man's voice spoke.

"We have your girlfriend," the voice said.

Daniel gripped the phone tightly, "I ... I don't have a girlfriend," he said.

"Yes you do. Tall, shoulder–length blonde hair, blue eyes, very attractive, goes by the name of Julia Jones."

"She's not my girlfriend," Daniel said, a slight panic in his voice as he spoke.

"No? Then you won't mind if we kill her ... slowly, will you?"

"What ... what do you want?"

"You know what we want. You have four hours to find her. After that, things are going to get very uncomfortable for your girlfriend here."

"Look! I ... I don't know ...!"

"Four hours! We'll call you then!"

"But ... wait!"

But the caller had already hung up.

Daniel slowly lowered his arm staring blankly, trying to remember something, anything that would tell him what those men were after. Julia's face came into his mind. He didn't know her, and yet, he couldn't just let her die, whoever she was. She had saved his life twice. Daniel brushed the thoughts away, then gazed down once again at what he'd found in the drawer.

A photograph of himself stared back up at him. It was attached to a file. He reached down and took the file out of the drawer, then walked back across the room and sat down in the armchair to look at it. He went through it carefully, reading the file. It seemed to be a complete file all about his life. As he reached the end, he saw other photographs. He took them out of the file one by one, looking at them. There was a photograph of him leaving his building, a photograph of him getting into his car, a photograph of his meeting with his ex-wife outside her house. He picked up the last photograph and studied it carefully. It was the photograph of him speaking with a man in the station café. Daniel recognized the man as the dead man he'd found in the warehouse who'd been tortured to death. Daniel stood up, went back over to the drawer and quickly went through the rest of the papers inside it. After a few moments, he came across a paper giving information about the orphanage where he'd grown up. He studied it, remembering his time at the orphanage. Why would anybody want to gather all of this information on him? he thought. As he lifted the paper, which was attached to another, he found one more photograph beneath it. He stared at the photograph curiously with a puzzled expression on his face. It was a photograph of a Chinese woman standing outside a Chinese restaurant.

"Who the hell is this?" Daniel whispered softly to himself. He checked the back of the photograph. There was a name, Lin, and a date, 12th November, 1995. Just next to the date were the words 'Hong Kong'.

"Hong Kong?" Daniel whispered to himself.

He turned the photograph back over and stared at it again, then he put it in his pocket and closed the secret drawer. He turned, went over to the sofa, put on up his black jacket, and headed for the door. There was another noise from the neighbours next door. The man and woman were shouting at each other again. Daniel sighed, thankful that they weren't 'his' neighbours, then slowly open the door and glanced out into the corridor. Once again, the corridor was empty. He stepped out, closed the door behind him and walked to the left towards the lift. As he reached it, he decided against it and turned to the stairs instead. He went through the door and into the stairwell, and was about to go downstairs when he heard a noise from down below. Daniel stopped, listening, then moved to the side to look down over the banisters. Two floors below, he saw a man's hand holding onto the banister. The man below coughed.

They were obviously watching the lifts as well as the stairs, Daniel thought. Slowly, he moved back away from the banister and turned, then, as quickly and as silently as he could, he began to walk up the stairwell. Daniel made no sound as he went and finally reached the top floor after a few minutes. He opened the door that led out onto the rooftop and went to the right. The rooftop was flat. He moved across it to the edge and looked down at the street far below. The wetness of the dark street shone beneath the dimly-lit yellow streetlamps that lined it. Just to the right of a building nearby, he could see a man waiting beside a car. Daniel moved back from the edge of the rooftop and looked around. He saw the rooftop of another building to his left, its height just a few feet lower than the rooftop on which he stood. He walked over to the rooftop's edge on the left to gaze down at the other rooftop just below his. Between the two buildings there was a space of about twelve feet. Daniel stared at the other rooftop, and then down at the alley between them far below.

He would have to jump, he thought.

He remained still, thinking. He thought of going back downstairs and blazing his way through the men waiting below with the gun Julia had left him. He would have the element of surprise, but he didn't know how many men were there. He would run the risk of getting himself killed, or getting taken alive and tortured, and then, who would save Julia? He took a deep breath, deciding that he had no choice but to jump. He took one last look down at the alley, then turned and walked back across the roof. When he felt that he had gone far enough, he turned to face the edge of the roof where he was going to jump. He paused, staring at it and breathing heavily, then he took one last deep breath and began his run towards the edge of the roof. He ran as fast as he could blocking out all thoughts from his mind, concentrating only on the roof's edge, and then, when he reached it, he jumped.

For a few moments, he seemed to be flying through the air, and then he landed with a loud grunt on the opposite rooftop and rolled to a stop. He remained still for a few moments, panting heavily, realizing that he'd made the jump successfully. He leaned forward to push himself up and a pain shot up his left leg. He grunted and continued to push himself up onto his feet, disregarding the pain. When he was standing, he limped across the roof towards the rooftop door.

Some minutes later, after taking the building's lift down to the ground floor, Daniel limped out of the building's back exit, careful to make sure that nobody saw him.

CHAPTER 10

The taxi stopped in the dimly-lit narrow street. Daniel paid the driver and stepped out. He closed the door and waited for the taxi to drive away before limping slightly a short distance along the street to where he'd seen his car parked. It was an old yellow Volkswagen Beetle. It stood out from the other parked cars on either side which were all more modern and had darker colours. As he reached it, he paused, looking around at the dimly-lit narrow street. A streetlamp nearby shone with a dim yellow light, its light reflecting on the wet rain-swept surface of the dark road on which he stood. Daniel remained looking around wondering why on earth he had parked his car there. Who was John Keaton and why had he met him in the café? And why had he taken a taxi to the warehouse instead of his own car? Other questions also ran through his mind like, who were the men who had beaten him? Who was Julia Jones? And why did she have a file on him? As his head began to spin with all of the questions running through his mind, he leaned against his car for support. He squeezed his eyes shut, trying to blot out everything, then turned, opened his car door and got in. He had to focus, he told himself, he had to focus. He glanced up at the dark brooding apartment buildings that rose up on either side of the narrow street, wondering if he'd come to see someone who lived in one of them. Once again, no answers came to him. This is where Julia Jones had found him, he thought. This is where he'd lain beaten in the road. He squeezed his eyes shut once more trying to remember. Various images flashed into his mind. There was the white light again, and someone crying out in pain.

"Aaaaaaargh!!"

Daniel jerked and opened his eyes.

The scream had been in his mind, and yet, it had seemed so real. Daniel breathed heavily as if he'd just run a few laps. He took one last look at the dimly-lit narrow street, then reached forward and started the car's engine. As he began to pull the car slowly away from the kerb, he noticed an envelope. It was a plain white envelope on the floor just in front of the passenger's seat. Daniel quickly stopped the car, then reached down and picked the envelope up. He switched on the car's interior light and stared at the envelope in his hand for a few seconds. The name Daniel McGlade was written on the front. The envelope had already been opened. Daniel looked inside and pulled out a letter. He opened it up and read what was written. There were only a few lines.

'Meet me at the station café at midday. Suzie's life is in danger'.

Daniel read it again, and then again. He stared at the letter in his hands hoping that if he stared at it long enough he might remember something. The letter was obviously the reason why he'd met John Keaton at the station café. But now there was another question. Who the hell was Suzie?

Daniel sighed, feeling frustrated, then put the letter back into the envelope, put the car in gear again, and drove towards the end of the narrow street.

*

Daniel's leg was feeling a little better as he limped along the corridor towards his apartment at the end. He had entered the building through the back entrance, carefully checking to make sure that no one was there waiting for him. A new pain in his side had begun to hurt, but he'd had worse he told himself. As he neared his apartment, he saw that the door was partly open. Daniel stopped. He took out his gun, then continued forward carefully. He reached the door and listened. Hearing no noise, he pushed it slightly inward, then went through into his apartment with his gun raised and ready. What he saw made him gasp in shock. His apartment had been completely ransacked. There were clothes, books, papers and other objects scattered everywhere on the living room floor. The floor was a mess. It was as if a mini-tornado had passed through his apartment leaving behind a destructive mess in its wake. Daniel limped slowly around the room, gazing down at the mess, and then slumped down in one of the two armchairs which hadn't been overturned. He sat for a moment, studying the mess on the floor in front of him, then stood up, took off his jacket, and went into the kitchen. He took out a can of beer, pulled it open and gulped the beer down as if he'd had an unquenchable thirst. When he finished, he wiped his mouth and looked once again at the mess. He limped across the living room, stepping around the mess on the floor, and went into the bathroom. He took off his clothes, stared into the mirror for a few moments at his bruises, then had a shower. When he was finished, he went into the bedroom, which he found was also a mess, and got himself into some clean clothes. He dressed all in black, as was his habit, transferred his wallet, his gun and other personal items to his fresh clothes, then looked into the mirror on the bedroom's dresser. The face that looked back at him was a mess, a real mess. There were bruises on his face and a cut over his left eye and another cut on his lip. He took out the gun, checked it again to see if it was loaded, even though he didn't need to, put the gun back in his holster, turned and limped back across the mess on the floor of his apartment and went out through the door.

*

The police station's lamp glowed above the dark brown stone entrance. Daniel limped up the steps. He was limping less, but still limping nevertheless. He stepped inside and went over to the station's desk and saw Sergeant Greene hunched over some papers and writing something down. Sergeant Greene, who was a bald-headed middle-aged man, looked up as Daniel approached the desk. The moment he saw Daniel, he frowned. He stared at Daniel's beaten face.

"Jesus! What happened to you?"

"Long story," Daniel said, leaning on the desk. "Tell Marshall I'm here."

"You mean Inspector Marshall Tiloni?"

"You know who the hell I mean!" Daniel said bitterly.

Sergeant Greene gestured towards an empty seat against the opposite wall, "Take a seat, I'll call him when I've finished with these papers."

Daniel leaned further onto the desk, staring into the desk Sergeant's eyes bitterly, "Look! It's a matter of life and death! I need to speak to him now!"

Sergeant Greene stared back at him, "I said ... take a seat!" Sergeant Greene said firmly.

Daniel remained staring at him for a moment, then turned abruptly and went over to the seat. He sat down between an elderly man holding a dog on his lap and a woman with a bruised face.

Daniel looked at the woman and smiled at her, "Your husband?" he asked.

"Damn right it was my husband!" the woman answered. "That creep!"

She looked at Daniel, observing the various bruises on his face

"Your wife?" she asked.

Daniel chuckled, "Yeah, she's pretty strong," he said.

The woman leaned back shaking her head.

"Marriage!" he said bitterly.

"Amen to that!" Daniel said, almost to himself.

He stared up at the clock on the wall. Three hours and ten minutes, he thought.

He leaned forward, "Hey!" he shouted across to Sergeant Greene. "Can you tell him to hurry up? This is a matter of life or death!"

"Patience McGlade!" Sergeant Greene shouted back. "You don't work here anymore! You don't give orders! All right?"

Daniel stared back at him with piercing cold eyes. The desk Sergeant glanced away and looked back down at his paperwork. Daniel sighed, frustrated at having to wait, then made a quick decision, stood up and headed for the staircase.

"Hey! Where do you think you're going?" Sergeant Greene shouted at him.

Daniel ignored him and started up the steps just as a young man about the same age as him started coming down the staircase.

"Daniel!" the young man said in surprise. "What the hell are you doing here?"

Daniel stopped on the staircase looking up at his friend Inspector Marshall Tiloni as he came down the staircase towards him.

"Marshall!" Daniel said, as the young Inspector reached him. "I've got to speak to you!"

"Can it wait? I'm on my way to …"

"Marshall, it can't wait! A girl's life is in danger!"

Inspector Marshall Tiloni stared at his friend's bruised face, "Hell Daniel! What the hell happened to you? Are you okay?"

Daniel nodded, "I'm okay. I need to talk to you! Right now!"

Marshall looked at him with a worried expression, then nodded, "Okay, let's go up to my office."

Sergeant Greene, who had pretended not to be listening, now watched them both as they went up the staircase to the offices above.

*

As they walked through the large open-plan office, other police officers sitting in their cubicles behind their desks stared a Daniel as he walked past. The whole office seemed to go still and silent. Daniel felt their eyes on him as he walked past. Finally, they reached Inspector Marshall Tiloni's office and went inside. Marshall walked around his desk and sat down behind it in his chair gesturing for Daniel to sit down in the chair facing him.

"Don't mind them," Marshall said, gesturing towards the open-plan office outside.

"Yeah, I know," Daniel said, slumping down in the chair in front of Marshall's desk. "They hate a dirty cop!"

Marshall leaned forward onto his desk looking at his friend, "Daniel, I never once believed the accusations against you! Hell, we were together for two years, you were my partner, my friend."

"Yeah, well you're in the minority!"

"The Chief didn't believe it either."

"Screw him!"

Daniel glanced around Marshall's office, "You've got your own office now, nice!"

Marshall grinned, "I've made some good busts," he said.

"I'll bet you have. You always were a good cop Marshall."

Marshall studied the bruises on Daniel's face, "Jesus man! What happened to you?"

"Problems," Daniel said.

"Why didn't you call me?"

"I lost my phone, your number was on it. Things have ... been moving fast."

Marshall nodded understandingly.

Daniel leaned forward towards him, "Look, Marshall, a girl's life is in danger. I've got just over three hours to give some people what they want, otherwise they're going to kill her!"

Marshall stared at him for a moment.

"What people?" he asked. "Give them what? And who's the girl? Jesus Daniel! What have you got yourself into?"

"I don't know."

"You don't know?"

"Look, I can't remember anything, at least, nothing about what's happened in the last few days."

Marshall continued to stare at him, "You ... you've lost your memory?"

Daniel nodded, "I can't remember a thing! I don't know who the girl is or who the guys are or what they want!" Daniel paused, "And … there's something else. There's also a body."

"A body?" Marshall repeated. "Whose body? Where?"

Daniel shrugged, "Some guy named John Keaton. Apparently I met him …"

"Apparently?"

Daniel slammed his fist down onto Marshall's desk, "Look! I said I can't remember! Okay?"

Marshall raised his hands in an effort to calm Daniel down.

"Okay, okay. So … tell me what happened. How and where was he killed?"

Images flashed into Daniel's mind once again.

"It … it was in a warehouse, a red-brick warehouse in the industrial suburb just outside of the city. He was …"

The image of John Keaton, bound hand and foot and half naked with electrical wires attached to his body came into Daniel's mind. He saw the man's face, trapped like still life in a horrible expression, a silent scream that no one would ever hear. Daniel shook his head, trying to shake the image from his mind.

"He … he was tortured with electricity," he said. "I guess the shock killed him. Anyway, there's nothing we can do for him now, you can send a patrol car there. But … the girl we can save! Her name's Julia Jones, she … she saved my life, I owe her."

Marshall leaned back in his chair still staring across at Daniel. He gave a long sigh, as if the story he'd just heard was too unbelievable to be true.

"Daniel, you … you don't remember anything about the past few days?"

Daniel sighed impatiently staring back across at him, "That's what I said!"

"It's just that … two days ago, you came in here to speak to the Chief. I wasn't here. I was out on a case, but the chief told me …"

Daniel sat up, suddenly becoming alert.

"Did he say what it was about?" Daniel asked.

Marshall shook his head, "No, he didn't say, but …"

Daniel stood up.

"Where is he? In his office?"

Marshall stood up and ran round the desk quickly to grab Daniel by the arm as he was reaching for the door.

"Daniel! The Chief is in a meeting!"

"Damn it Marshall!" Daniel said, pulling Marshall's hand away from his arm, "A girl is in danger! I've got three hours left to find her! I need your help!"

Marshall raised his hands again.

"Okay, okay Daniel. I'll go see the Chief, tell him it's urgent. You ... you wait here, okay?"

Daniel stared at him, then glanced down and shook his head, "Marshall, I ... I'm sorry ... I didn't mean to ..."

Marshall squeezed Daniel's shoulder, "It's okay, it's okay. I'll tell the Chief you're here."

Marshall gestured back towards the chair in front of the desk.

"Sit down and wait here, I'll be back in a few minutes."

Daniel nodded, looking at his friend, then stepped back towards the chair and sat down.

"Two minutes," Marshall said as he opened his office door, and then he was gone.

Daniel sat alone in the office. The sound of the activity coming from the large open-plan office outside was muted by the frosted glass window behind him. Daniel leaned forward, looking at the photograph of Janet, Marshall's girlfriend, on the desk. Some things never change, Daniel thought, studying the picture. Before, when he was still in the police force, he, Marshall and Janet spent some time together after Daniel's divorce. He knew that they'd felt sorry for him and were trying to cheer him up. Janet was a good kid, attractive, simple, she didn't ask for much, and yet, she was always there for others. A smile broke onto Daniel's face as he picked up the picture and stared at it. Marshall was lucky, really lucky, he thought. Marshall seemed to have everything, at least, everything that he himself didn't have. He placed the photograph back down just as the door behind him opened. Daniel turned and saw police Captain Jeff Turner walk into the room followed by Marshall. The Chief, everybody called him 'Chief' although he was really a Captain, was in his late fifties with thinning grey hair and was a little on the plump side. Nobody had ever dared to call him fat. Marshall closed the door behind them as the Chief stood with his arms folded staring down at Daniel.

"Jesus! Look at you! Did you fight with an express train?"

Daniel stood up.

"Marshall told me your story," the Chief said. "We've got someone checking up on your Julia Jones, and the body you found, John Keaton. I've sent a patrol car to check the warehouse out where you say his body was"

"Tell them to be careful," Daniel said. "Those guys may be around and they're dangerous."

Marshall nodded. He was about to leave the office when Daniel reached into his pocket, "Hey! See if you can find anything on this Chinese woman," Daniel said, handing him the photograph he'd found in the file.

Marshall took the photo, glanced at it and then left the office.

"What the hell have you got yourself into now?" the Chief asked, staring at Daniel.

Daniel shrugged, "I don't know. I can't remember the last few days."

"Yeah, Marshall told me."

The Chief moved forward and sat down on the corner of Marshall's desk."

Daniel sat back down in the chair.

"Marshall told me that I came here a few days ago," Daniel said, looking up at the Chief.

"That's right."

"What was it about?"

The Chief pointed at Daniel's head, "You must have got a pretty hard bump!"

Daniel shrugged, "Hard enough I guess. Why was I here?"

The Chief stared down at him for a few moments before speaking.

"You were asking after a girl, a Chinese girl. You said her name was Suzie."

"Suzie?" Daniel repeated, a puzzled expression now on his face as he lowered his head and tried to remember.

"Yeah, that's right. You called her Suzie Q," the Chief chuckled. "At first, I thought you were asking about a song, thought you were stoned or high or something."

"Suzie Q?" Daniel repeated again, trying desperately to remember. "Did you find out anything about her?"

The Chief shook his head, "I came up zilch. You said she'd been in the city for just a few days as she came in illegally with a false name."

"Did I say why I was looking for her?"

"Nope. You refused to tell me anything, just said that it was important to find her."

Daniel stared thoughtfully for a moment.

"A Chinese woman called Lin," he said. "And now a Chinese girl called Suzie Q. They asked me … they asked me where 'she' was."

"Who's they?"

"The guys at the warehouse, the one's who did this," Daniel gestured to his beaten face.

The Chief scratched his head, "Well, you say a man's dead, a girl's been kidnapped and in danger of being killed, I'd say this Suzie Q, whoever she is, is important to someone."

Daniel leaned forward onto the desk beside the chief, "If only I could remember!" he said through gritted teeth. "Damn it! I don't remember anything!"

He hit the desk.

The door opened and Marshall came back in. He glanced down at Daniel and handed him back the photo of the Chinese woman.

"I made a copy," he said, then he turned to the Chief, "A second patrol car joined the first," Marshall said. "They were already near the area and went in as soon as they got the call. They've searched it and found nothing, it was completely empty. No body, no guys, no nothing. If they were there, they've vanished."

"If …?" Daniel began to say staring up at him. "Hey! Do you think I'm making this up?"

Marshall raised his hands in defense, "Sorry, I didn't mean to say it like that. I'm sure they were there."

"What about Julia Jones and the Chinese woman?" the Chief asked.

Marshall shook his head, "Nothing," he answered. "As for Mr. John Keaton … apparently he's been missing for two days. I checked him out, he seems to be just another insurance man."

Marshall paused, his eyes looking sympathetic as he gazed down at Daniel, "We'll do all we can to help," he said.

Daniel looked up at the clock, checking the time.

"Less than three hours left," he said. "We've got to find Suzie Q, who-ever she is!"

"We'll do all we can," the Chief said, staring down at him. "You look terrible, why don't you go home, get some rest and leave this to us?"

Daniel looked up at him, then shook his head.

"Rest? Are you joking? That girl saved my life! Twice!"

The Chief shrugged, "Do you have any other leads?" he asked.

Daniel glanced up at the second hand ticking slowly around the clock, then shook his head again.

"No, but … I can't just leave it!"

Suddenly, a thought came to him.

He clicked his fingers, "Maybe … just maybe one lead!" he said.

He looked up at the clock.

"I've got to go!" he said quickly, then he stood up and made for the door.

"Hey! Where are you going?" the Chief asked.

"To follow up on one lead!" Daniel said, glancing back at him.

"Hey Daniel!" Marshall said, holding out a card with his name and number on it, "Here's my number again. Don't lose it this time, and stay in contact!"

Daniel nodded, taking the card, "Thanks," he said.

"And Daniel?" the Chief said, just as Daniel opened the door.

Daniel turned to look at him.

"I'll tell you what I told you a few days ago," the Chief said. "I never believed you took that money."

Daniel stared at him for a moment, then nodded.

"Thanks," he said again, then he went out and closed the door behind him.

CHAPTER 11

The drive through the city took Daniel to the older part of town. It was late and there were few cars so he made good time. As he parked his car nearby a well-known Chinese restaurant, he checked his watch. He had two hours and forty-five minutes left to find the girl, whoever or wherever she was. As he stepped out of the car, Daniel couldn't help wondering why a young Chinese girl would be so important to some people. There was a chill in the air and a breeze that threatened to bring more rain. Daniel glanced up at the night sky, there was not a star in sight. He pulled the lapels of his jacket up and crossed the street towards the restaurant feeling better in his leg. He was barely limping now. Two Chinese men glanced at him as he passed them heading for the restaurant. It had been a long time since Daniel had been to Chinatown, at least, as far as he could remember. As he walked, he had the feeling that the two men he'd passed were looking back and observing him carefully. They had glanced at him, and he'd heard them speaking softly in Chinese as he had passed them. Daniel took no notice and didn't look back but continued on and entered the Chinese restaurant.

Because of the late hour, there were only a few customers sitting at the tables. Chang, the Chinese manager who always had a welcoming ready smile, came over to him.

"Mister Daniel McGlade!" he said, in a rather thick Chinese accent. "So good to see you again! So glad you could once again visit my humble establishment! But … what happened to you?" he asked, gazing at Daniel's bruised face.

Daniel shrugged, "I had an accident with a gorilla," he said.

Chang looked at him in surprise, "Oh! A gorilla!" he said, trying to understand.

He smiled again, gesturing around the restaurant, "As you can see, it is so late, and normally we will close as soon as the last customers finish eating, but for you Mr. McGlade, maybe we can …"

Daniel shook his head, smiling, "No need to do me any favours Chang. I haven't come to eat.."

"Oh?" Chang said, looking at Daniel curiously.

"I'm here to see Wang," Daniel said.

"Ah! Mr. Wang!"

Chang shook his head, keeping his smile as he did so, "Very sorry Mr. McGlade. Mr. Wang busy man! Work all day! He tired now, gone to bed."

"Yeah? Well, wake him up!"

Chang chuckled, "Mr. McGlade is joke, yes?"

"No," Daniel said, looking at him.

Chang's smile faded a little as he noticed the determination in Daniel's face. Suddenly, a phone buzzed in Chang's pocket and Chang took it out.

"Yes?" he said into the phone.

Chang listened, then began to speak rapidly in Chinese.

As Chang was speaking, Daniel looked around the restaurant at the few customers eating. At one table there was a family speaking softly in Chinese and laughing. Daniel noticed three waiters eyeing him carefully, one had moved behind the bar and was obviously reaching for a gun in case there was going to be some trouble. Chang finished speaking on the phone and put it back in his pocket. His smile returned as he looked once again at Daniel.

"Mr. Wang say you may go up to his office. He is waiting for you. I will show you ..."

Daniel brushed past him, "I know the way," he said.

He stared at the waiters menacingly as he walked across the restaurant to the backroom behind a thick black curtain. He entered a short dimly-lit corridor, then took the steps up to the first floor. A big hefty looking Chinese guy with a slight beard barred his way at the top of the stairs. As Daniel reached him, he stared directly into the big guy's eyes. A man's voice came from behind the big guy, breaking the momentary silence.

"Let him pass Yak," the voice said.

Yak moved aside, his eyes still staring piercingly into Daniel's.

As Daniel passed him, he saw Mr. Wang standing in an open doorway which led to his office.

Mr. Wang smiled, "Daniel McGlade," he said. "Your visits are always … a surprise."

He gestured behind him to his office, "Please, come in."

Daniel said nothing as he moved past him and entered the office. It was a large office, lavishly furnished with Chinese style furniture mixed with comfortable modern armchairs and a sofa. To the right was a mini-bar and on the wall next to the bar was a huge flat TV screen fixed to the wall. Daniel walked over to Wang's large desk which was black and well polished and sat down in the chair in front of it. Wang, who had closed the door, after gesturing for Yak to step inside the room, walked over to his desk and sat down in the comfortable chair behind it. It was a chair which seemed fit for an Emperor.

"Don't be alarmed by Yak's presence," Wang said, gazing across at Daniel with a smile on his face. "I never go anywhere without him these days, he's a great bodyguard."

Yak took up position beside the door staring silently and impassively at Daniel.

"Does he speak?" Daniel asked, gazing back at Yak and looking the big guy up and down.

Wang chuckled, "Rarely," he said.

Although it was late, Wang was still wearing a smart dark suit, white shirt and a patterned red tie. As Daniel observed him, he thought that he looked like a businessman, a rich businessman who was used to getting his own way. Although his smile seemed genuine, Daniel felt sure that it wasn't.

"Sorry to get you up out of bed," Daniel said.

Wang's smile widened into a grin, "As you can see, I was already up," he said. He leaned back in his chair staring across at Daniel carefully, "So, Chang said you looked a little, er … battered, and he was right. You must be frequenting some very bad people McGlade, but please tell me that this has nothing to do with me."

Daniel remained silent for a moment, staring back across at Wang, then he reached for his pocket. Yak cried out and immediately stepped forward. Daniel pulled out a photo and Wang raised his hand for Yang to stop moving forward and gestured for him to go back to the door. Daniel threw the photo down onto Wang's desk.

"Do you know her?" he asked.

Wang glanced down at the photo. He stared at the photo of the Chinese woman called Lin for a long moment, then slowly picked it up and studied it in silence, his face completely expressionless.

"Never seen her before in my life," he said finally, throwing the photo back down on the desk.

"Are you sure?" Daniel asked, watching him carefully.

Wang nodded, "Sure,"

Daniel picked up the photo and put it back in his pocket.

"What about a girl named Suzie Q? Ever hear of her?"

Wang chuckled, "Isn't that a song?"

"In this case, it's a girl," Daniel said. "A Chinese girl."

Wang pursed his lips thoughtfully, then shook his head, "Sorry, I can't help you Inspector … oh! It's not Inspector anymore, is it? You're not a cop anymore, are you?"

"That's right," Daniel said, eyeing him carefully.

"Yes," Wang said, with a smile on his face. "So unfortunate. You had such a promising career."

"Well, I'm a private detective now … but I'm sure you already know that."

Wang shrugged with a grin, "Word gets around," he said.

He leaned forward in his chair, "Well, now if there's nothing more on your mind, I'll have Yak here show you out."

"How's the drug business?" Daniel asked with a smile.

Wang's face suddenly became very serious.

"We don't do drugs McGlade, nor anything else illegal. We're a respectable business now, but you should already know that, right?"

"Right," Daniel said, staring back at Wang intensely. "If I find out you've been lying to me Wang, I'll be back!"

Daniel stood up.

"Hey!" Wang called out after him as Daniel turned and headed back towards the door, "You're not a cop anymore, remember?"

Daniel reached the big guy and stared up into his eyes. Yak stared back down at him in silence, then moved away from the door to let Daniel pass. As Daniel opened the door to leave, he suddenly turned.

"By the way, do you know a John Keaton? Or a Julia Jones?"

Wang chuckled again as he looked across at Daniel standing by the door, "My, my, you really are looking for a lot of people."

"Do you know them?" Daniel repeated, his voice sounding a little harsher.

Wang shook his head, "Never heard of them either," he said.

"Thanks! You've been a real help!'" Daniel said sarcastically.

"Anytime!" Wang said, waving goodbye.

As Daniel left, going out of the door followed by Yak, Wang's expression changed. He suddenly became very serious. He took out his mobile phone and dialed a number.

"Chang?" he said. "Get someone to follow McGlade! He's leaving right now!"

CHAPTER 12

Daniel left the restaurant and pulled the lapels of his jacket back up against the night's chill. As he walked across the road and got into his car, a man stepped out of the restaurant and got into a nearby car to follow him. Daniel sat behind the steering wheel thinking, then took out the name card he'd taken from John Keaton's dead body. He studied the address, then started the car's engine and pulled away from the kerb. Behind him, at a safe distance, another car's lights came on and also pulled away from the kerb beginning to follow him. As Daniel made his way through the city's rain-soaked neon-lit streets, the car behind followed him all the way, keeping well back.

Candwell, on the other side of the city, was a quiet up-market residential area bordering on the western suburbs. The streets were lined with comfortable looking well-kept houses with wide green lawns stretching from the houses down to the tree-lined road in front of them. Daniel drove slowly, glancing at the houses and checking the numbers until he came to the house that he was looking for and then parked his car a few houses past it on the opposite side of the road. Daniel sat, looking across at the house for a moment, then got out of his car. He glanced around both left and right as he walked across the road towards it. It was late, and the suburban street was hush quiet with nobody else in sight. He stepped up onto the pavement on the other side and walked across the lawn towards the house, continuing to glance around as he went. The house was in complete darkness. Somewhere farther down the street, a dog started barking, disturbing the silence of the night. Daniel reached the house. He was sure that there was no one at home, especially as he'd seen the body of the occupant, John Keaton, who had been tortured to death. But he could have a wife or a girlfriend, Daniel thought, he had no way of knowing. He cursed himself for not being prepared, wishing that he had asked Marshall for more details about Keaton. Daniel stopped in front of the front door and pressed the doorbell. He waited for a few moments then pressed it again. No one came. Daniel looked carefully around behind him at the road and at the nearby houses, then he reached for something in his pocket. Glancing around one more time, he knelt down in front of the door and started picking the door's lock. It took less than a minute before the lock clicked and then the door opened. Daniel pocketed his lock-pick, then pushed the door open wider. He stood up and quickly entered, closing the door behind him. He remained still, listening, then reached into another pocket and brought out a small torch which he turned on. Remaining still, he shone the beam around the hall in which he found himself. Directly opposite him was a staircase leading up, probably to the bedroom, or bedrooms, Daniel thought. He shone the beam of light to the right and saw the living room. It was neither too large, nor too small, just conveniently comfortable. Daniel stepped into the living room and quickly went over to the windows to draw the curtains. He turned and shone the torch's light around the room. He saw the door to the kitchen which was slightly open. Daniel shone his light onto a desk which was in a far corner. He went over to it and looked through the drawers but found nothing of importance. As he leaned up, he glanced at the laptop which was on the desk. He sat down in the swivel chair in front of it and turned it on. A few seconds passed by, then the screen came to life and asked him for the password to enter. Daniel leaned back in the chair looking around on the desk for a picture of Keaton's family or friends, hopefully with a name written on the back, but there were no photos there. Too easy anyway, Daniel thought to himself. He took the card he'd found on Keaton's body out of his pocket and shone the torch down onto it looking for a possible clue to a password. As he read the card, he heard a creaking sound behind him.

Floorboards, Daniel thought stiffening, someone creeping … trying not to make a sound …

Daniel suddenly spun round in the chair and saw a man standing a few feet away from him. In the darkness, Daniel could only make out the man's shape. The man looked big. Daniel leapt up out of the chair as the man quickly moved forward to lunge at him. Daniel avoided the lunge and moved to his right to roll over on the floor. He quickly got up onto his feet and the man turned to face him, his hands reaching out towards Daniel to grab him. Daniel avoided the hands, raised his fists in boxing style and landed a left jab straight into the man's face. The man staggered back and Daniel moved forward following with another left jab and then a right. The man cried out as blood began to spout from his nose. Daniel feigned another left jab then punched the man square on the jaw with his right making the man fall back onto the floor with another cry. Another man appeared from the shadows running at Daniel. Daniel grunted from the impact of the man's body and fell back onto the floor with the second man's weight on top of him. The man swung a fist down and caught Daniel in the face, he swung another fist down but Daniel managed to avoid it. He reached up for the man's throat, grabbed it and squeezed hard. The man started to choke grabbing at Daniel's hands, then Daniel threw him to the right, rose up, and slammed a fist down into the man's stomach. The man lay gasping for air. Daniel was just getting up onto his feet when the first man, who in the meantime had picked up the laptop, smashed it down onto Daniel's head. Daniel cried out and fell back down to the floor.

"Hey! Come on!" he heard the man shout out as he lay dazed in the semi-darkness of the room. He heard the second man still gasping for air as the first man helped him up onto his feet.

"I got the laptop!" the first man said. "Let's go! Come on!"

Daniel heard the scuffling of feet as they moved past him heading towards the door. He forced himself up onto his knees as he heard the door open. The crack to his head felt as if it had split his skull open. He placed a hand to his head and with his other hand on the desk, pushed himself up onto his feet knocking things off the desk as he did so. Daniel glanced towards the front door and saw out in the hall that it was open. He took out his gun then forced himself to run across the room, stumbling into an armchair as he went. When he reached the door, he managed to see the two men scrambling into a car parked in the road further along to the right. Daniel ran from the house and across the lawn heading for his own car as he heard the engine of the men's car starting up. Daniel reached his car just as the other car pulled away fast from the kerb. Daniel jumped into his car and started the engine, then gunned his car forward giving chase to the men's car in front. Behind him, he didn't notice the other car which turned on its lights and began to follow him as it had done from the restaurant in Chinatown, only this time the speed was much faster, much, much faster.

CHAPTER 13

The men in the car in front were aware that they were being chased.

They drove fast through the dark city streets turning this way and that, speeding through the red lights and skidding around corners trying to lose Daniel who seemed to be sticking behind them like glue, following their every move.

"Faster!" the man in the passenger seat said, glancing back towards Daniel's car as Daniel screeched his car around a corner almost skidding in his attempt to keep up with them.

"I'm going as fast as I can!" the other man said. "What do you want me to do? Wrap the car around a lamp-post?"

The man in the passenger seat took out his gun and lowered the window. As the car skidded around another corner the man was thrown against the door.

"Jesus!" he breathed.

He leaned out of the window and aimed his gun at Daniel's car which was chasing them behind. Daniel swerved his car to the left as the man fired. The bullet missed. Daniel almost skidded out of control, then managed to put the car back on track and gunned it forward after the men's car in front.

"Who the hell is this guy?" the man behind the wheel of the car in front said.

"Hold her steady!" the other man leaning out of the window shouted. He fired his gun again. Once again, the bullet missed. This time Daniel didn't swerve the car to avoid the bullet, instead, he took out his own gun and fired at the men's car. The bullet hit the back window smashing it to pieces.

"Jesus Christ!" the man behind the wheel shouted.

He jerked the car to the left and sped over a bump in the road causing the man leaning out of the window to lose his gun.

"Hell!" he cried out.

"We're headed for the railroad!" the man behind the wheel shouted.

The other man brought himself back in from the window breathing heavily.

"We gotta lose this guy!" he said.

"I got a better idea!" the man behind the wheel said.

He gunned his car through a barrier leading to the railroad, which was on the outskirts of the city and drove across the various railroad tracks. The car almost flew off the ground as it bumped off the tracks at fast speed. Daniel slowed down as he saw the tracks in front of him but his speed was still fast and the first bump of the tracks made his car rise up and crash down before speeding over the other tracks. The men's car, farther across the tracks in front, had stopped. From the railroad lighting shining down onto the tracks from both sides, Daniel could see the men getting out of the car. Daniel turned his car so that the car's side was facing their position and quickly got out gripping his gun tightly in his hand.

The first shot whizzed past him making him duck behind his car, another two shots hit the body of his car on the side facing the men. Daniel returned fire, once, twice, three times, as more shots rang out and bullets whizzed past him or imbedded themselves in his car.

"Hey! Is that you McGlade?" one of the men shouted out.

Daniel stopped firing.

"Who wants to know?" he shouted back.

"Very funny McGlade! Let's just say, we're the guys who've got your girl! Let us go and she'll be safe! If anything happens to us, she's dead!"

Daniel remained silent, thinking.

"How do I know you won't kill her anyway?" he shouted back.

"You give us what we want, and we'll let her go!"

"Is it the Chinese girl you want? Suzie Q?"

"You know what we want!"

"What's she to you?"

"No questions McGlade! Just give us the Chinese chick!"

Daniel stood up from behind his car and looked across at them.

"Who the hell are you?" he asked.

The two men stood up. The man in front with the gun, who had been driving the car, grinned, "That's for us to know, and for you to die for if you try to find out!"

For a few moments, the men stared towards each other in silence, then an ear-blasting sound of a horn came from their right. Daniel looked to his left and saw the light of a train speeding along the tracks. The men turned towards the oncoming train, but it was too late. Both men screamed and turned vainly to shield their bodies with their arms, and then the train hit them and smashed into their car causing it to burst into flames as the men's bodies were thrown across the tracks from the force of the speeding train, their bodies flying through the air as if they were merely lifeless puppets. Daniel watched as the train's brakes screeched to slow down and come to a stop. After a few seconds of standing in silent shock, Daniel ran across the tracks to the wreckage of the blazing car. He glanced down at the body of one of the men which was badly burned and terribly disfigured. As he neared the car, the heat of the flames forced him back. The door which had been left open was now nothing more than a twisted piece of metal. Just inside, Daniel could see the laptop. It was damaged and bent out of shape. Daniel wrapped a handkerchief around his right hand, took off his jacket and put it over his head, took a deep breath, then lunged forward for what was left of the laptop on the floor of the car. Wincing in the heat, and with flames all around him, Daniel managed to quickly reach in and grab it. Even through the handkerchief he'd wrapped around his hand, he could feel the heat of the laptop stinging his flesh as he quickly pulled it out of the car. The laptop fell to the ground and he picked it up running back away from the car, then he dropped it again and fell to his knees taking off the jacket from over his head and beating it on the ground to put out the flames. A few seconds later, after the flames had gone from his jacket, he leaned forward onto the ground and breathed a sigh of relief. He looked down at the damaged laptop which lay just a few feet from him, then glanced back up at the blazing car. Men were shouting and running back from the train towards him and the car. Daniel got to his feet, picked up the damaged laptop using his jacket as a protection against the heat, and walked away from the blazing car and back across the tracks to his own. Far across, on the other side of the tracks, a man stood beside a car nearby the now broken gate. He observed Daniel carefully and spoke rapidly into his mobile phone. The language he spoke in was Chinese.

By the time Daniel had driven back across the tracks and reached the gate, the Chinese man and his car had already gone. Daniel drove with his left hand on the steering wheel, the pain from the heat of the laptop still stinging his right hand. He felt tired, no, exhausted. Questions tumbled over and over in his mind as he drove. Behind him, a car pulled out from a side street and once again began to follow him. Too tired to even notice, Daniel drove through the darkened city streets followed by the car behind.

CHAPTER 14

The room was dark.

A woman sat across the table from the girl sitting opposite. The girl could barely see the face of the woman in the darkness. A light shone down onto the large mahogany table from above, lighting up only the table beneath it and the woman's hands which were placed on the table's top.

"When McGlade brings us the girl," the woman said, "he must be eliminated."

"I understand," the girl said.

"I have chosen you because of your profile. I assume you have no problem with your orders?"

"No problem," the girl said.

"Good," the woman said, a satisfied tone to her voice. "I have full confidence in you. Failure is not a word we like to use in our organization."

The girl nodded, although the woman sitting across from her could barely see it.

"I understand," the girl said. "I will not fail you. You may consider McGlade already dead."

*

Daniel sat in the office leaning forward with his arms on the desk in front of him and his head on his arms. His eyes were closed. He wished that he could sleep, wipe away the fog that was forming in his mind impeaching clear thoughts. The office door behind him opened and Marshall walked in.

Daniel looked up.

"How's the laptop?" he asked. "Could they get anything from it?"

Marshall sat down behind his desk.

"Not much I'm afraid. A few pieces here and there."

"Like what?"

Marshall shrugged, "There's some mention of a spider on it."

"A spider?" Daniel repeated incredulously.

"We don't know what it means. We're looking into it. We did get something back on the license plate number you gave us though, the car belonged to a company called Wayman Industries.

Daniel glanced down thoughtfully.

"Wayman ..." he said quietly to himself.

Suddenly, he reached into his pocket and brought out a card.

"What is it?" Marshall asked as Daniel stared down at the card in his hands.

"John Keaton," he said. "The man I found dead in the warehouse, he worked for Wayman."

"But ... I thought he was in insurance."

"Wayman Industries, Wayman Insurance, maybe it's the same company. It's too much of a coincidence that they have the same name."

Suddenly the door opened.

A young detective named Rice entered and glanced down at Daniel before speaking to Marshall.

"We Got a make on the description of those two guys you were looking for."

He threw two mug shots down onto Marshall's desk.

"Daniel, this is Detective Terry Rice," Marshall said, gesturing up towards the young detective. "He's my new partner."

Daniel looked at the young detective and nodded, "Is he showing you the ropes?" he asked.

Detective Rice nodded back with a grin, "Well, we've only just started working together, but …yeah, yeah, he is."

"Well you're in good hands," Daniel said, leaning forward to look down at the photos on the desk, "Marshall's a good cop."

"Is that them?" Marshall asked, gazing down at the photos as Daniel examined them.

Daniel studded them for a moment, then nodded, "That's them," he said.

"The big guy is Stone," Rice said. "And the little guy with the scar is Lewis. Jerry 'knife' Lewis. They work together, almost like brothers."

"Are you sure they're not the two guys who got killed at the railroad?" Marshall asked.

Daniel shook his head, "No, they were two different guys. When you're able to identify them you'll see they're not the same. These two guys here," Daniel pointed down at the photos in front of him, "were the ones I told you about who were beating me up at the warehouse. There was a third guy too, kind of non-descript, but he wore a smart suit."

"They're boss?" Marshall said.

Daniel shrugged, "Maybe."

"Anyway," Rice continued, "these two guys are from out of town. There's some kind of connection between them and a guy called Heller, Jack Heller, a former mob boss. Heller was never charged with anything, and to all accounts he's now going straight and running a meat factory down near the dock area. However, there is 'talk' that he's still in the game, and with acquaintances like Stone and Lewis, it seems likely that he is. Apparently, even bad guys in this city avoid Heller, and what they call, his 'gang'."

Daniel stared thoughtfully down at the photos, "Jack Heller?" he said, with a note of surprise to his voice.

Rice nodded.

Marshall sighed, leaning forward onto his desk, "It looks like Heller's drafted in some muscle," he said. "We've been trying to get something on Heller for a long time."

Daniel glanced up at the clock on the wall.

"Only one hour and forty minutes left," he said.

The Chief suddenly appeared at the door.

"What's going on?" he asked.

The three men looked at him.

"I'm sorry," Marshall said. "You were in a meeting. We got some info on the guys who beat up Daniel and probably murdered another guy, John Keaton."

"That other guy," the Chief said. "There was no body."

"We think Heller's involved," Daniel said, standing up to face the Chief.

"And there's something about a company called Wayman Industries," Marshall said.

The Chief raised his eyebrows.

"Wayman Industries?" he said. "That's a pretty important company."

"Two other men have been killed," Marshall said. "Daniel ..."

"Daniel?" the Chief repeated, turning to stare directly into Daniel's eyes. "You're beginning to leave a trail of bodies!"

"That's what happens when people try to kill you," Daniel said.

The Chief nodded, "Right. And can you tell me Daniel, why are these people trying to kill you? Just why are people being killed?"

"How do I know?" Daniel said bitterly, staring back into the Chief's eyes.

"Look!" Daniel said. "We've got less than two hours to find the girl, or they're going to kill her!"

He turned to Marshall, "You check with Heller, I'm going to Wayman Industries."

"Hey!" the Chief said, staring at him. "You're not a cop anymore! And you sure as hell don't give orders to my men   !"

Daniel turned and stared back into the Chief's eyes showing a snarl on his face as he spoke, "A girl is going to be killed in less than two hours if we don't do anything! And when I say 'we', that means me, and you! The police!"

The Chief shrugged, "Okay. Marshall and Rice can check out Wayman Industries …"

"No! Wayman's mine!" Daniel said.

The chief chuckled, "Not looking like that it's not," he said, pointing at Daniel's battered appearance. "Looking like that, you'd do better looking into Heller's gang. I'll send a squad car with you …"

"Don't bother!" Daniel said, cutting off his sentence.

He turned to Marshall, "Be careful!" he said. "And if she's there, at Wayman's, bring her back alive!"

He turned, stared once more at the Chief, then brushed past him and left the office.

CHAPTER 15

Jack Heller, former gangster boss for a mob in an east coast city, now ran what was seemingly a respectable business. The police however, suspected that he was still involved in some shady dealings, although nothing could be proven. He ran his business from an office in a large meat-packing warehouse down near the docks.

Daniel parked his car two streets away and checked his gun. He sat for a moment looking around at the darkened street, then got out and walked towards the warehouse. A full moon shone high in the sky, its reflection shining on the calm dark waters in front of the docks. Daniel glanced at the two large boats moored to the docks as he walked past them, keeping well into the shadows and away from the dock's overhead lights. Daniel approached the large warehouse which loomed up in front of him, dark and foreboding as if it were a silent monster waiting to devour all who neared it. Daniel thought about trying the front entrance, then decided against it. He ran around to the side of the building and found a side door. To his surprise, it was open. He took out his gun, holding it ready, then slowly went inside closing the door silently behind him. Not all of the warehouse lights were on, but the few that were showed various machines and stacked packing boxes which covered the large warehouse floor.

To the left, at the far end of the warehouse, he saw the cold room which was used for storing the meat, to the right was a metal staircase leading up to two offices. Both of the office lights were on. Daniel moved forward carefully towards the staircase. As he neared it, he could hear voices coming from the offices above him. Daniel paused for a few moments, hiding behind a packing machine and trying to hear what the voices were saying, but he was too far away. As he moved forward, he brushed against a box which toppled over and fell to the floor. Daniel froze and moved back behind the machine again as a door to one of the offices opened and a man came out. The man stood still, gazing down over the warehouse floor for a moment, then he turned and went back into the office without closing the door.

"It's nothing," Daniel heard the man say.

Daniel moved out from behind the machine and went closer, positioning himself beneath the stairs.

"We've got to find her before they do!" Daniel heard another man say.

Daniel recognized the voice, it was Jack Heller, whom Daniel had met a few times when he was still in the police force. Daniel had been investigating a murder at the time, but nothing could be proven against Heller or his gang.

"The guy we found at the warehouse didn't know," another man said, "otherwise he would have talked … believe me, he would have talked."

"I brought you in from out of town to do a job!" Heller said, angrily, "and so far, all you've given me is a dead body!"

"The guy you called McGlade, he's the one who knows," said another man. "At least, as far as the dead guy was able to tell us before he died."

"McGlade?" Heller repeated bitterly. "And you had him!"

"He would have talked too," the other man said, "if that girl hadn't shown up."

"And where are they now?" Heller asked.

"We don't know," the other man said. "We went to McGlade's home, turned it upside down, but didn't find anything. We've been out there looking for them, but came up with nothing."

Daniel moved forward and started to go slowly up the staircase keeping his gun ready to fire.

"Damn it!" he heard Heller shout as Heller slammed his fist down onto his desk and stood up from his chair. "I paid you a lot of money to …!"

He suddenly stopped and looked to the right. Daniel was standing in the open doorway with his gun aimed directly at Heller's head. The other men turned and stared at Daniel in surprise.

"McGlade …" Heller whispered to himself, staring across at Daniel with an expression of complete disbelief. Daniel stared directly back at Heller, who was standing behind his desk, then glanced quickly at the three men, two of whom he recognized from the other warehouse, standing in front of him. A tall man he'd never seen before was staring at him intensely.

Suddenly, the mobile phone on Heller's desk rang breaking the silence. The ringing continued for a moment with no one moving.

"Answer it!" Daniel said finally, staring at Heller.

Heller, who'd raised his hands, slowly lowered them, then he picked up his phone.

"Yeah?" he said, into the phone.

There was a moment's silence as he listened, then he glanced at Daniel.

"He's already here," Heller said.

Daniel moved forward around the side of the desk and held out his left hand towards him while keeping his gun aimed at them with his right.

"Give me the phone," he said.

Slowly, Heller stepped forward and handed Daniel the phone.

Daniel put it to his ear, "Who is this?" he asked.

There was a moment of silence at the other end and then the connection was broken.

"Who was that?" Daniel asked, staring at Heller.

"You think I'd tell you?" Heller replied.

Daniel glanced down at the phone and saw that the number wasn't shown.

Heller grinned, "He uses a private number. Good luck finding out who it was."

Daniel stared back at him. Heller was a big man in his fifties with white hair. There was a calm air of confidence about him. The sleeves of the white shirt he was wearing were rolled up as if he were about to do some manual work, but he wore a smart red tie, open at the neck, as if he still wasn't really used to wearing them.

"I guess you know who it was, don't you?" Heller said after a moment.

Daniel stared at him, a hatred burning inside him, "The guy who framed me for taking bribes," he said.

Daniel raised his gun, aiming it directly between Heller's eyes.

"I ought to kill you right now! No judge, no jury!"

Heller remained calm as he shrugged, "Then you'd never find out who it was, would you?"

"Where's the girl?" Daniel said.

One of the other men, the smartly dressed one who Daniel had remembered as the third man who'd been with Stone and 'Knife' in the warehouse basement, started sweating. From the corners of his eyes Daniel noticed his hands begin to shake.

"You won't shoot me," Heller said very calmly, too calmly for Daniel.

"Where's the girl?" Daniel asked again.

Heller sighed as if he were disappointed, then lowered his arms and sat down on the corner of his desk.

"You know … I was hoping 'you'd' tell me that," he said. "It seems we're looking for the same thing."

Daniel continued to stare at him, aiming his gun directly at him.

"What do you mean?"

"The Chinese girl. You had her, we know you did. What happened? Did you lose her? Oh … yes! You can't remember, can you? At least, that's what my men tell me."

He chuckled, "You know, I didn't believe it at the time, but now …"

"Where … is …. Julia … Jones?" Daniel said, accenting every word for effect.

Heller gazed back at him with a puzzled expression.

"Who?" he asked.

"Julia Jones!" Daniel repeated, raising his voice in anger.

Heller stared back at him with a blank expression.

Daniel grimaced, showing his teeth, "Blonde, about five foot nine, pretty! She's not someone you could forget!"

Heller glanced across at his men, "Do you know who he's talking about?" he asked.

The third man in the smart clothes with his arms still raised looked back at him, "Sounds like the chick who helped him to escape," he said.

"Oh," Heller said, with an understanding nod. He glanced back at Daniel.

"We don't know who she is," he shrugged. "We didn't take her. I promise, we're only interested in the Chinese girl."

Daniel continued to stare at him.

"Why?" he asked. "You tortured and killed a man because of this girl!"

Heller glanced once again at his men, then back at Daniel.

"You mean … the man my men found almost dead in the warehouse?" he shook his head, "Sorry, but that wasn't us. According to my men, they found him like that, already tortured apparently, he died just a few minutes later."

"That's right!" the third man in the smart suit said, looking towards Daniel with his arms still raised.

A sneer came onto Daniel's face, "Who are you kidding? That was just your style!"

Heller chuckled again, "You know, things have changed since you left the force. Believe it or not, we're not in the murdering business anymore. I run a legitimate business now."

"A legitimate business? Is that why you're looking for the Chinese girl? Why your men tied me to a chair, beat me up and almost tortured me too?"

Heller glanced at his men, then sighed shaking his head, "That was … regrettable." He stared across at both Stone and 'Knife'. "Is that true?" he asked.

There was an embarrassed silence, then 'Knife' lowered his arms and shrugged, "We were just trying to get you the information you wanted," he said defensively.

Heller shook his head again and looked at Daniel, "Hired help from out of town!" he said, with a disappointed tone to his voice. He shrugged, "What can you do? I'm sorry."

He sighed again, then continued, "Now, it's true we're looking for the Chinese girl, but someone else is looking for her too, and whoever they are, they're the ones who killed the guy at the warehouse, not my men."

"Give me one reason why I should believe you!" Daniel said.

Heller smiled folding his arms comfortably as he gazed back at Daniel.

"Now, why would I lie when I have the upper hand?" he asked.

He nodded towards the open door behind Daniel. Daniel spun round and saw a fourth man now standing in the open doorway behind him. The man had a scar down the left side of his face and was aiming a gun directly towards him.

"Lower your gun, nice and easy," the man said.

Slowly, Daniel lowered his gun.

'Knife' stepped forward and quickly took the gun from Daniel's hand.

Stone, the big guy, came over and stood in front of Daniel, staring into his eyes.

"Do we kill him now boss?" he asked.

Heller shook his head, "Tsk, tsk."

He stared at Stone as if he couldn't believe his ears.

"Boys, boys, boys … what did I tell you?"

He glanced at Daniel with an apologetic smile, "You see what they sent me to work with?" he sighed, shaking his head, "Good help is getting hard to come by these days!"

He looked at the man called 'Knife', "Lower your gun you moron!" he shouted. "You're making 'me' nervous!"

"But …" Knife began to say, pointing at Daniel.

"Lower it!" Heller shouted louder.

Reluctantly, Knife lowered his gun. Heller got off the desk, took Daniel's gun out of Knife's hand and handed it back to Daniel.

Daniel hesitated, staring at him in disbelief, then took his gun.

Heller smiled at him, "Want a drink?" he asked.

Daniel stared at Heller in surprise as Heller walked back around his
desk to a mini-bar on the far side. Daniel remained still, watching him
as Heller chose a drink and began to pour it into two glasses. Daniel
continued to observe him, not knowing what to make of this new pre-
dicament, then slowly, he put his gun away.

"Just soda water, right?" Heller said, coming back towards him and
holding out a glass.

"How did you know?" Daniel asked, once again surprised.

Heller shrugged, "I know a lot about you. I like whisky myself, but just
this once I'll join you in a soda water."

Heller gestured towards a chair, "Please, take a seat."

Daniel glanced at the other four men who were standing staring at him,
he hesitated once more, then he stepped over to the chair and sat down.

"I'm sorry you lost your job," Heller said, sitting down in the chair
behind his desk. "You were a good cop, that wasn't supposed to happen."

"Are you going to tell me who your someone was?" Daniel asked, nodding at Heller's mobile phone lying on his desk.

"Or rather … is?" he added.

Heller shook his head, "That's one thing that's confidential, I hope you
understand."

Daniel stared back at him, then sipped his drink.

"As for the Chinese girl, Suzie Q, or so I'm told her name is," Heller continued, "that's a different matter. We both seem to be looking for her. We know you had her."

"And why is she so important?"

Heller shrugged, "Let's just say … there's a lot of money involved."

"In the legitimate business now, huh?" Daniel said, wryly.

Heller shrugged again, "You know, one goes off the track from time to time, for the right price."

"Okay, let's say I believe you, you said there was someone else involved, who are they?"

Heller leaned forward, gazing down into his drink, "We … don't know much about them, other than the fact that they're dangerous. We believe they killed the guy at the warehouse, we believe they had you, that's where you got most of your bruises from, not us."

"He gave me a few," Daniel said, gesturing with his glass towards the big man called Stone, who remained standing staring down at him with the other three men.

Heller gave Stone a bad look, then glanced back at Daniel, "Sorry," he said. "Like I said, good hired help is hard to come by these days. We believe you escaped from them, but … the other guy … well, he wasn't so lucky. And now, unfortunately, you can't remember a thing about what happened."

Daniel sat thinking for a moment, "What do you know about something called Spider?" he asked.

Heller gazed down at his drink for a moment, then looked back up at Daniel, "We've heard rumours," he said. "About an organization called Spider. A secret organization. Do you think that's who these guys are?"

Daniel nodded, "It's possible," he said. "How did you find out about the Chinese girl?"

"A guy came to us, wanting to sell us some information. He said it was worth a lot of money. Just find a Chinese girl named Suzie Q he said, and also something about a butterfly."

"A butterfly?" Daniel repeated.

Heller shrugged, "Yeah, we don't know what the butterfly is, anyway … there's a buyer if we find both."

"A buyer?" Daniel said. "For a Chinese girl with a butterfly?"

Heller shrugged, "That's right."

"And … what if they want to kill this girl?"

Heller glanced down once more, thinking about it carefully, "I thought about that," he said finally. "I want to find the girl first, then I'll decide what to do." "You'd sell her for money?" Daniel asked.

Heller shook his head, "Didn't say that," he said. "Look, we can work together, we can pool our resources, find the Chinese girl, find out what these other guys want …"

"And I'm supposed to trust you?" Daniel said incredulously.

Heller nodded, "I know, I know. I haven't always been lily-white. But believe me, we can work together on this."

Daniel looked at the clock on the office wall.

"I've got someone to save," he said. "I'm wasting my time here."

He stood up.

"At least give me your card," Heller said. "A private eye has a card, right?"

Daniel looked at him for a moment, then reached into his pocket and handed him a card.

Heller smiled, "Thanks," he said, taking the card.

Daniel turned to leave, then saw the huge form of Stone barring his way to the door. Daniel stopped in front of him and looked up into Stone's eyes. Stone stared down at him with a cold expression on his face. Suddenly, Daniel hit him in the stomach. It was so fast that Stone had no time to react. He doubled over, clutching at his stomach and trying to catch his breath, then Daniel shot a fist to his face, then another, and Stone went down to the floor, first onto his knees, and then he fell onto his side.

Daniel glanced back at Heller, "I owed him that," he said.

Heller nodded with a smile, "I'm sure you did," he said. "Good luck ... saving a life."

Daniel nodded, then glanced coldly at Knife who was looking at him in both surprise and shock as if he were seeing him for the first time. Daniel thought about taking his knife from him and putting it to his throat, then decided against it, turned and left the office.

Heller leaned forward onto his desk, his arms folded as he glanced down at the huge form of Stone now lying unconscious on the floor.

"You know, I saw that kid fight once," Heller said. "He used to be a boxer before he joined the police. They called him 'The Black Cat'"

"The Black Cat?" repeated the man in the smart suit.

"Yeah," Heller said. "On account of he would always bounce back up if he was knocked down. Some people said he had nine lives. He was also fast and packed a pretty good punch."

"I've never seen anyone best Stone like that!" Knife said, staring down wide-eyed at his unconscious partner on the floor.

"Were you serious what you said boss?" the man in the smart suit said. "About working together? You know how much that Chinese chick is worth!"

Heller glanced down at Daniel's card in his hand.

He shrugged, "Maybe," he said. "Then again, maybe not."

CHAPTER 16

Just as Daniel was getting into his car, he received a call on his mobile phone. He sat down behind the wheel of his car thinking about his conversation with Heller, then answered it.

"Hello?"

"Danny?"

Daniel recognized Marshall's voice on the phone.

"Marshall?"

"Yeah, listen. Those guys from the railroad, we got a make on one of them. His name was Barker. Jimmy Barker. He worked for a company called Weelstein."

"Weelstein?" Daniel repeated, running the name quickly through his mind and trying to remember if he'd heard of it before.

"And get this," Marshall continued. "Weelstein is a company that is connected to Wayman. They're office is even in the same building. I'm on my way to Wayman's now with Rice. Did you see Heller?"

"Yeah, I saw him."

"How'd it go?"

"It's a dead end, at least, that's how it looks. Hey, look, I know what the Chief said, but I want to go to Wayman's."

"Hey Daniel, why don't you let Rice and me …"

"I'm coming!" Daniel said. "Wait for me!"

Daniel turned off his phone, then started the engine of his car and began driving across the city towards the address of Wayman Industries. At that time of night, the city looked like a ghost town, there wasn't a soul around. Daniel sped through the empty city streets, gunning his car on as fast as it would go towards the other side of the vast coastal city.

*

Wayman headquarters was a huge building in an important part of the city. It was surrounded by a fence and had a large metal gate that opened electronically in front. Next to the gate was a guard-post. A uniformed guard was sitting in the small cubicle next to the gate reading a book. Daniel sat observing the building through the fence from his parked car in the road which passed by outside. He turned, seeing the headlights of another car coming along the road towards him. The car drew up beside him and he saw Marshall and Rice sitting in front of an unmarked police car. Daniel got out of his car and got into the back of the police car.

"You got here fast!" Marshall said back to him.

"We don't have much time," Daniel said.

Marshall nodded, "Right … so, how do you want to do this?" he asked.

"Just get me in," Daniel said.

"Okay," Marshall said, nodding. "Lay low so the guard doesn't see you."

Marshall gestured for Rice to drive up to the gate. Rice drove the car forward slowly then turned it towards the large metal gate and stopped beside the guard's cubicle. The guard glanced up from his book and stood up. He stepped to the window and glanced out. Marshall noticed the surprised look on the guard's face as he stared out through his window and down at the police badge that Marshall was holding up towards him.

"Er … yeah?" he said nervously.

Marshall leaned his head out of the car window.

"We had a complaint," Marshall said.

"A complaint?" the guard repeated. "What kind of complaint?"

Marshall shrugged, "It wasn't clear. They just said that something wasn't right."

The guard spoke with surprise in his voice, "What … what do you mean not right?"

"Hey look," Marshall said. "I don't know, all right? The desk Sergeant said to come out here and check it out, so here we are. Is anybody inside?"

"Just … just a few office workers," the guard said, still sounding nervous.

"Okay if we go in and look around?" Marshall asked.

The guard put his hand to his mouth, "Well … maybe I should phone …"

"Hey look," Marshall said. "It's probably a crank call, we'll be quick, okay?"

The guard thought for a moment, then nodded, "Okay, you … you just wait right there."

He went to the back of his cubicle, picked up the phone and spoke to someone. A few moments later, he was back at the window with a nervous smile on his face.

"You can go right on through," he said.

He pressed a button and the barrier in front of the car lifted.

"Thanks," Marshall called out as Rice drove through and into the grounds beyond.

They drove in the darkness along the driveway which led up to the huge main building. A few of the lights in the main building were on. A few other smaller buildings stood on either side of the central building in darkness. Marshall glanced back looking down at Daniel who was lying out of sight on the floor behind him.

"Now," Marshall said.

Daniel nodded, "See you outside," he said, then opened the door of the car as Rice slowed down almost to a stop to let Daniel out. Daniel got out and closed the backdoor quietly, then ran away from the driveway into the darkness and among the trees beyond the carefully cut lawn.

The unmarked police car continued on, rolled slowly up to the main building and stopped outside it. Both Marshall and Rice got out and made their way across the parking area and up the steps to the main door of the building. Before they had even reached the last step, the large twin doors in front of them opened up allowing a wide shaft of light to flood out from the interior and engulf them in its brightness. As both men adjusted their eyes, they saw a tall, thin, sophisticated-looking woman gazing calmly towards them from inside. She was wearing a sleek black gown and although she was probably in her forties, she looked younger and still had an attractiveness about her.

"I understand that you have a problem officers?" the woman said in a soft sultry sounding voice as they reached her.

"Er … yes," Marshall said.

He glanced at Rice who was now standing beside him, but Rice merely glanced back and said nothing.

Marshall tried a smile.

"Er ... we had a call about a disturbance at this address.."

He shrugged, "Probably just a crank call, but we have to check, you understand?"

The woman's calm manner as she stared at him was beginning to make him feel nervous.

The woman nodded, "Of course, you must do your work officers, that is only natural. My name is Miss Clarke, I am one of the founders of this enterprise."

She stepped aside for them to pass.

"Please, come in."

As Marshall and Rice stepped on through, they found themselves in a huge well-lit hall with a marble floor and a small fountain in its centre, its water trickling peacefully. There was a wide red-carpeted staircase that led upstairs and copies of statues and reprints of famous paintings which decorated the hall.

"You may look around if you wish," Miss Clarke said. "I'm sure you will find nothing. As you so aptly put it Inspector, you probably had a crank call."

Marshall looked at her, she was standing stiffly, motionless, just as if she were part of the hall's scenery, as if she herself were a statue. Marshall walked forward looking around with Rice beside him.

"What's upstairs?" Marshall asked, pointing to the staircase.

"Offices," Miss Clarke said calmly. "A few private chambers, in case someone would wish to stay over."

Marshall turned and looked at her, "Anyone else here?" he asked.

"Just a few office workers and myself."

"Mind if I look upstairs?" Marshall asked.

"You may look where you wish Inspector," Miss Clarke said. "We have nothing to hide here."

Marshall turned to Rice, "You take this floor and the basement," he said.

Rice nodded and walked away.

"By the way," Marshall said, turning back to Miss Clarke as he began to walk towards the staircase, "Are any of your employees missing?"

Miss Clarke stared back impassively, then shook her head.

"Not that I am aware of," she said.

"What about a John Keaton? Ring any bells?"

Miss Clarke glanced down suddenly, then her eyes came back up as she composed herself once more.

"We have many employees Inspector. I'm not in a position to know all of their names. But … as far as I am concerned, not one of our employees is missing."

Marshall continued to look at her in silence. A few seconds passed, then he spoke again, "You might want to look into it," he said, then he turned towards the staircase.

"Rest assured Inspector, I will," Miss Clarke said, remaining still and watching Marshall as he reached the staircase to start going up.

*

Outside, Daniel was running past some bushes in the darkness towards the back of the huge building. He reached a door and tried it, but it was locked. He knelt down, took something from his pocket and placed it in the lock. He moved it around inside and within a few moments there was a click as and the door sprung open. Carefully, he pushed the door further open and then stepped inside taking out his gun. He found himself in a long and dark corridor. He took out a small torch and shone its beam along the corridor in front of him. He walked forward with slow careful steps glancing into the various rooms which lined the corridor on either side as he went. He appeared to be in some kind of storage area. Boxes were piled high in many of the rooms he looked into. Finally, he reached the end of the corridor and followed it around to the right. As he turned he saw a light at the far end. He paused, gripping his gun tightly, then, raising his gun at hip level, he moved slowly forward. A door at the far end was partly open shining light into the darkened corridor. As he reached the door, he turned off his torch and put it away. Still gripping his gun tightly, he pushed the door slowly forward with his other hand. The door creaked slightly in the silence as it open wider. Daniel stepped in through the open doorway glancing around. Various machines, computers and screens filled the room. Desk consoles were filled with various coloured buttons and switches as lights on the consoles flashed on and off. Daniel was impressed. He stood looking around at the all of the machinery wondering just what it was the company was doing. A noise sounded to his left and instinctively he crouched down behind one of the machines. Two men came into view, one of them was wearing a white coat as if he were a doctor or a scientist. The other man was wearing a normal dark suit. Both men were talking, and as they came nearer, Daniel began to hear what they were saying.

"When will it be ready?" the man in the suit asked, stopping nearby one of the machines with various flashing lights.

"Well … that depends when you find the girl," the man in the white coat said.

"Okay, let's say we find her tonight."

"One day, maybe two days. But … 'after' you find the girl."

"Don't worry, we'll find her."

"You'd better. This whole operation depends on you finding the girl, if not, some people are going to be very displeased."

"Hey, we're working on it, okay?"

Suddenly, Daniel's mobile message tone sounded.

"Hell!" Daniel whispered to himself under his breath. He quickly reached for the phone and turned it off.

"What was that?" the man with the white coat said, gazing around the room.

The other man pulled out a gun.

"Someone's here," he said.

He motioned for the man in the white coat to remain still, then moved slowly forward holding his gun ready to fire. The man in the white coat remained still, watching the other man as he moved slowly forward between the machines and the consoles with the flashing lights.

"Who's there?" the man in the suit called out. "Come out and show yourself!"

Daniel waited until the man was almost upon him, then he leapt out and threw himself against the other man knocking him into a machine that was behind him. The man's gun dropped from his hand and clattered to the floor, and before the man could react, Daniel hit him on the head with his own gun hearing a crack as his gun butt hit the man's skull. The man crumpled to the floor like a lifeless puppet. Quickly, Daniel turned and aimed his gun at the man in the white coat. The man raised his hands, his eyes wide open in fear as he stared at the barrel of Daniel's gun which was aimed towards him.

"Don't shoot! Don't shoot!" the man said nervously.

Daniel walked over to him keeping his gun aimed at the man's head.

"Who ... who are you?" the man in the white coat stammered.

"Never mind that," Daniel said. "Where's the girl? Where's Julia Jones?"

The man shook his head, "I … I'm only a scientist! Don't shoot me, Please!"

"I said, where's the girl?" Daniel repeated, with annoyance in his tone.

Suddenly, the scientist looked at Daniel as if he were seeing him for the first time.

"You … you're him! You're him, aren't you? The … the man they call 'The black Cat'."

Daniel moved closer and pressed his gun up under the man's chin.

"Nice to know I'm famous," he said. "Now, where's the girl?"

"B … b… basement!" the man stammered, his fear of being shot very visible as he now began shaking uncontrollably.

Daniel grinned at him, but his grin was unpleasant, making the scientist believe that without a doubt, he was indeed capable of pulling the trigger.

"Lead the way," Daniel said.

CHAPTER 17

Marshall walked back down the staircase checking his phone to see if there was a return message from Daniel. Just a few minutes earlier he'd sent a message to say that he and Rice were leaving and would be waiting for him outside. He frowned when he saw no return message, then put away his phone. Miss Clarke was standing in the hall watching him as he descended the steps of the staircase. She stood completely still, as if she had not moved an inch since he had left her to check the rooms upstairs. All he'd found were empty offices, but he hadn't checked them all, the place was too large and it would take too long, but what he had done was give Daniel enough time to get into the building, hopefully without being noticed. Rice appeared from the side of the staircase as Marshall reached the final steps.

"Nothing," Rice said, looking at Marshall as he came to a stop.

"Sorry to have disturbed you," Marshall said, walking over to Miss Clarke.

Miss Clarke smiled at him coldly.

"No problem Inspector. Now, if you'll let me get back to my work …"

"You're working at this time of night?" Marshall asked.

Miss Carke smiled slightly.

"In another part of the world, it is already morning Inspector. My work is rarely finished."

Marshall observed her for a moment. Beside him, Rice seemed to shuffle from one foot to the other as if he were impatient to leave,

"Don't forget to look into that employee of yours," Marshall said.

"Mr. John Keaton," Miss Clarke said with no emotion in her voice. "I will do so Inspector." She gestured towards the door, "Now, if you don't mind …"

Marshall gave her a curt nod, "Of course. Good night," he said

Rice nodded goodbye to Miss Clarke and quietly followed Marshall out.

"What do you think?" Rice asked, as they walked towards the unmarked police car.

Marshall glanced back at Miss Clarke who was now standing in the open doorway watching them leave.

"I think something's not right," he said.

"What makes you think that?" Rice asked as they reached the car.

Marshall glanced across the roof of the car at Rice as he opened the car door.

"Call it a gut instinct," he said.

They both got into the car and Rice started the engine.

"So … what do we do now?" Rice asked.

"We wait," Marshall said, staring through the car window at Miss Clarke who was now closing the door. "We wait outside for Daniel to come out."

"And if he doesn't?" Rice asked.

"Then we come back with a search warrant," Marshall said.

                                  *

The scientist was still visibly shaking as he led Daniel down into the basement. The basement was well lit and clean and looked like it was used as just another storage room. Boxes were piled high everywhere.

"There's nothing here!" Daniel said through clenched teeth. "If you're lying to me …!"

"No! No! Please! She's here! She's here! There … there's a secret entrance! A special door!"

"A secret door, huh?" Daniel said, pushing the scientist across the floor of the basement. "Where is it?" he asked, his voice sounding impatient.

"It … it … it's over there! Over there!" the scientist stuttered, pointing towards the far end of the basement.

Daniel followed behind, his gun trained on the scientist's back as he went. When they finally reached the far wall, the scientist stopped.

"Okay, where is it?" Daniel asked, looking around for a door. "There's no door here!"

"I … I … s … said it was a 'secret' door." The scientist said, shaking and stuttering with his hands still raised high.

The scientist led him over to a pile of black metal boxes stacked against the wall.

"It … it's here!" he said, reaching behind one of the boxes.

He touched something behind the box and Daniel heard a 'click'. Suddenly, the wall began to move, or at least, part of it. Daniel stood back and stared at the wall as it moved aside to reveal a secret passageway with steps leading down. Daniel remained still, staring at the passageway for a few seconds, then moved forward and prodded the scientist in the back with his gun.

"Move forward," he said. "Any tricks and you're the first to be shot, understand?"

The scientist nodded quickly, moving forward through the open wall doorway, "I … I understand!" he answered nervously.

Daniel followed him down the steps. When they reached the bottom they came to a dark tunnel with red lights running along the walls on either side. They walked quietly along it, then turned a bend which led to the left. The tunnel stretched further along, its red lights giving the darkened tunnel an eerie, macabre effect. As they neared a partly open door at the end of the tunnel, Daniel heard voices. He grabbed the scientist in front of him, forcing his to stop. He listened, then slowly he pushed the scientist forward towards the door.

"Make one sound," Daniel whispered to the scientist, "and you're dead. You get that?"

The scientist nodded nervously, feeling the barrel of the gun pressed into his back. Together, they moved slowly forward. When the scientist was just inches away from the door, Daniel pushed him against the wall keeping his gun pressed into the man's back, then he leaned forward and looked through the gap of the partly open door. He heard voices coming from inside. He listened, then he heard the voice of Julia Jones. Through the gap in the partly open door he saw no one. He had to take a chance, he decided. He turned, grabbed the scientist, then pushed him through the door. Daniel quickly stepped in behind him, using the scientist as a shield in case anyone fired in his direction. Julia, who was sitting on a chair, turned and saw Daniel behind the scientist. She gasped in surprise, staring at him with wide eyes. The man who'd been asking her questions turned and stared at Daniel in stunned shock.

"Hello Julia," Daniel said. "Are you okay?"

At first, Julia hesitated, then she nodded, "Ye ... yes," she managed to say. "How ... how did you find me?"

Daniel glanced around the basement. There were large screens on the walls, and computers, and machines with various consoles with switches and coloured buttons which flashed on and off. The equipment in the room seemed similar to the equipment in the room upstairs, except for the screens on the walls which seemed much larger. On one of the screens Daniel saw the image of Marshall's unmarked police car parked in the street outside the company's gates. He glanced at Julia and noticed that she wasn't bound to the chair she was sitting on.

"What's going on here Julia?" he asked.

Julia merely stared across at him, a surprised look on her face. The man who'd been asking her questions was tall and thin with sharp unpleasant looking features.

"So, you've decided to come to us McGlade," he said, matter of factly.

Daniel looked at him, then glanced back down at Julia.

"Julia?" he said, still waiting for her answer to his question.

"Julia won't be answering any questions," a woman's voice said.

The voice came from behind, causing Daniel to spin quickly around.

"Drop the gun!" the woman said, pointing a gun directly at him.

"You'd better do as she says," the thin man said.

Daniel glanced back at him. He saw the gun the man was now holding in his hand.

"Drop it!" the man said.

Daniel paused, staring at the gun the man had aimed at him, then let go of his gun and heard it clatter to the floor at his feet.

"I … I … didn't mean to … to bring him down here!" the scientist stuttered nervously as he glanced at both the man and the woman on either side of him. "He … he made me!"

"Shut up!" the thin man said.

"Your friend outside is very curious about us,' Miss Clarke said calmly, gazing across at Daniel. "I suppose we have you to thank for that."

A young girl suddenly appeared behind Miss Clarke wearing what could only be described as a sexy outfit, even though she was dressed like a punk. Like Daniel, her clothes were all in black. She had shoulder-length black hair, and her bright blue eyes shone beneath the fringe which hung down almost over them. Daniel stared at her, there was something about her face which was extremely pretty, but it was more than her natural beauty, there was something about her that attracted him. Daniel guessed that she was in her mid-twenties. He did not know why, but he couldn't stop looking at her. It was as if she had a power over him, some strange hypnotic power. The punk girl stared back at Daniel with a smile.

"Pick up his gun!" the thin man said, gesturing to the scientist.

The scientist scurried forward and picked up the gun that Daniel had dropped to the floor.

"Can I kill him now?" the punk girl said, leaning onto Miss Clarke and staring with interest at Daniel. The way she had spoken was almost like a purr, as if she were a cat.

"Not now Felicity," Miss Clarke said. "You know we need him alive, at least, for now."

"And … after?" Felicity asked, continuing to stare at Daniel with interest.

"After … you can do with him whatever you like," Miss Clarke said.

Felicity grinned, placing a finger to her lips as if she were a child, "Mmmmmm, then maybe … I'll kill him slowly," she said. "Very, very … slowly."

"Felicity seems to like you," Miss Clarke said to Daniel with a smile.

The thin man came forward and stood in front of Daniel, his gun trained on Daniel's stomach.

"Where's the Chinese girl?" he asked. "Suzie Q as you call her."

Daniel broke his gaze away from Felicity to look at him.

"I've no idea," he said, shaking his head.

"Still can't remember, eh?" the thin man said.

Daniel stared back at him with a grin, then shook his head.

"Even if I did remember," he said, with clenched teeth, "I wouldn't tell you!"

The man took out a phone and dialed a number.

"Forget the trap," the man said into the phone. "We have McGlade here, but without the girl."

He listened for a moment.

"Okay," he said, then turned off his phone.

He glanced towards Julia, who was now standing up from her chair and looking across at them.

"Looks like your plan didn't work!" he said to her.

Daniel turned to look back at Julia.

"Julia? What …?"

The gun butt hit Daniel sharply across the head before he could say another word. Daniel grunted from the pain and fell to the floor.

"Pick him up!" Daniel heard the thin man say above him.

Somebody grasped his arms as the basement room began to spin in front of Daniel's eyes.

"Take him to the car! We have to leave!" he heard the man say.

Daniel felt himself being lifted up off the basement floor. Coloured lights from the consoles seemed to be spinning around him as if he were being carried through some psychedelic corridor, and then he felt himself floating, floating among the colours, as he lapsed into unconsciousness.

CHAPTER 18

Slap!

Daniel grunted.

Another slap!

Daniel grunted again.

His face stung.

He moved his head, then opened his eyes.

Motion.

He was moving.

Darkness.

The sound of a car's engine.

Daniel realized that his head was leaning against a window.

He looked out.

He saw the image of a man in uniform through the window of a cubicle. The man was staring at Daniel strangely.

A barrier was being raised.

Daniel realized he was in a car going through the gate leaving the grounds of the company.

"He's awake!" a man's voice said.

"He'd better be," said another.

Daniel glanced in front of him and saw an ugly face of a huge man with a broken nose peering back at him from the seat in front. The driver beside him kept his eyes on the road straight ahead. The car turned to the left. As he glanced out of the window, Daniel managed to see the unmarked police car parked on the other side of the road with both Marshall and Rice inside.

"Where the hell is he going?" Marshall said in shocked surprise as he noticed Daniel sitting in the back seat of the expensive looking black company car. Another similar car followed behind the first. In the back seat, he saw a man sitting next to Miss Clarke.

"Follow them!" Marshall said, turning to Rice.

Rice started the car's engine, then pulled the unmarked police car out away from the kerb and began to follow the two cars along the street.

*

"Are you all right?" said a girl's voice beside Daniel.

Daniel turned his head and grunted feeling a sharp pain on the top of his skull. He touched his head gingerly, then looked at Julia Jones who was sitting on the back seat beside him.

"Wha ... what happened?" he asked.

"Baines hit you on the head," Julia said.

"Baines?" Daniel repeated. "The thin guy? Is that his name?"

Julia nodded, "Yes."

"It seemed like the woman was the one giving the orders," Daniel said, still holding his head and wincing.

Julia nodded, "That's Miss Clarke," she said. "She ... she's in charge of this section."

"This ... section?" Daniel repeated, trying to understand, his head still spinning slightly.

He stared out of the car window. Passing streetlamps glowed yellow one after the other as they drove past them along the street.

"Where ... where are we going?" he asked, wincing as he touched the bump on his head.

"I ... I don't know," Julia said.

Daniel looked at her.

Julia looked back at him, then glanced quickly away from his eyes.

Daniel stared at her thoughtfully for a moment, then turned and leaned forward towards the front seats.

"Hey!" he said to the two men in front. "Where are we going?"

The huge ugly guy turned to look back at him, "You'll find out when we get there!" he said.

Daniel stared at him, then leaned back in his seat.

"Real unfriendly types," he commented.

Suddenly, the driver put his foot down on the pedal picking up speed as they approached a bend in the road. The car went around the bend then turned quickly to the left leaving the road and entered a dirt road leading into a wooded area. The driver stopped the car, turned off the lights and looked behind. The other car which had been following behind them carried on along the road passing the dirt road. A few seconds later, the unmarked police car carrying Marshall and Rice also went past following the other car.

"Lost them!" the driver said to his partner with a grin. "They'll follow the other car all the way to the airport!"

Daniel suddenly realized what had happened. He leaned forward again, "Hey, look …"

The ugly guy turned and pointed a gun at him, "I've got orders not to kill you," he said. "But I'll shoot you in the knee if I have to!"

Daniel leaned back again.

"You still want to know where the Chinese girl is, right?" Daniel asked.

The ugly guy grinned, "And you still don't remember? We've tried the soft way to get you to remember, now we're going to try the hard way. After just ten minutes with us, you'll be dying to remember!"

"Miss Clark said that there was to be no torture!" Julia said.

"Well, maybe Miss Clark changed her mind," the man said with a grin.

The driver backed the car out onto the road and started driving back the way they had come.

"Your torture didn't work on that other man!" Julia said.

"That's because he didn't know anything. If he'd known something, believe me, he'd have talked! You were there! He was crying and begging for us to kill him at the end!"

"You killed him!" Julia said.

"Nah, he wasn't dead when we left him! Just unconscious! But ... you're right, we would have killed him if we hadn't been disturbed. We don't like to leave loose ends. Just like your boyfriend here. He's gonna die a slow death If he don't remember nothing! So, it's in his interest to remember!"

"Doesn't," Daniel mumbled.

"What?" the man said, looking back at him.

"Doesn't remember anything," Daniel said, looking at him, "Didn't they teach you anything at school?"

Daniel leaned forward towards him, "Not only are you uneducated, but you're one big ugly …!"

Suddenly Daniel grabbed the man's gun.

"Hey!" the man shouted, struggling against Daniel.

The gun let out a shot and the bullet went through the roof of the car. Daniel struggled against the big man trying to pull the gun away from him. Suddenly, the gun went off again, this time the bullet hit the driver whose head seemed to explode, falling against the window in a bloody mess. The car spun out of control, veered to the left, went off the road and crashed straight into a tree. The shock pushed Daniel and Julia forward against the front seats. Both of them remained still for a moment, then Daniel moved, opened the door on his side and fell out onto the ground. Julia grunted holding her head. She reached for the handle to the car door on her side but the car door wouldn't open. Still holding her head, she crawled across the back seat and fell out of the car and onto the ground beside Daniel who was beginning to stand up. Daniel moved around to the front of the car and looked through the windscreen at the two men who'd been sitting in front. The big man had gone head first through the windshield, shards of glass covered his bloody face. Both men were dead. Daniel opened the front door and searched in the men's pockets for a mobile phone but the only phone he found had been broken in the crash. He took the two guns from the men's bodies, put them in his pockets, then turned and staggered back to Julia. Julia had raised herself up onto her knees and was still holding her head. Daniel bent down, grabbed her arm and helped her up.

"Can you walk?" he asked.

Julia nodded slightly, "I … I think so," she said.

"Good. It's quite a walk, but I've got my car back there," Daniel said, pointing back down the road.

"Maybe … maybe I should wait here," Julia said. "You can come back …"

"Oh no!" Daniel said, staring at her closely. "You're coming with me!"

He grabbed her arm and pushed her in front of him.

"Hey!" Julia said, glaring at him. She saw the determined look in his eyes and quickly glanced away from them, then, without another word, she turned around and started to walk back to the road. They left the woods and began the long walk back along the road together, both of them in complete silence.

CHAPTER 19

Daniel's apartment still looked a mess. He took some ice out of the ice box in the kitchen, wrapped it in a cloth, and handed it to Julia who was sitting on the sofa. He sat down beside her and placed some ice on the bump on his head, wincing as he did so.

"Your place is a real mess," Julia said, glancing around at the living room.

"Yeah," Daniel said. "I'm firing the cleaning lady tomorrow."

He looked at her.

"Let me see that," he said.

Julia took her hand away from her head.

He studied her head.

"Nothing to worry about," he said. "It's just a scratch."

"Just a scratch?" Julia repeated. "Do you think it will leave a scar?"

Daniel shrugged, "Maybe, but don't worry, it'll make you look more manly."

Julia groaned touching her head, "You know just what to say to a girl, don't you?"

"I've had years of practice!" Daniel said. "So ... are you ready to tell me?"

"Tell you what?" Julia asked.

"Don't play games," Daniel said. "You weren't being held hostage, were you? You're working for them, right?"

Julia glanced at him, then looked back down at the floor.

"What's going on Julia?" Daniel asked. "Who are these people? Who are you? Is Julia Jones even your real name?"

Julia was about to speak, then she hesitated. She stood up and walked over to the open window-door which led out onto the balcony. She stood in the open doorway, staring out into the darkness and feeling the breeze of the ocean air wash all over her. She breathed the air in as if she were breathing in the sweet scent of perfumed flowers, then she stepped outside onto the balcony and gazed down at the waves crashing up onto the beach far below in the darkness. Daniel stepped out onto the balcony and stood beside her, observing her closely.

"It's beautiful here," Julia said, continuing to gaze down at the waves below.

"That's why I choose to live here," Daniel said.

"Isn't it expensive?"

Daniel continued to observe her.

"I never took a bribe, if that's what you mean," he said.

Julia turned to him, "I … I didn't mean …"

"Yes you did," Daniel said, looking directly into her eyes. "If you must know, one of my first clients was rich, he was pleased with my work, gave me a hefty sum of money."

Daniel remained looking at her as Julia averted her eyes from his gaze.

"Now you," Daniel said. "And no lies."

Julia hesitated once more, then sighed.

"I … I'm not supposed to … I'm not supposed to tell anyone!"

"Hey!" Daniel said, reaching forward and lifting up her chin so that her eyes looked into his. "I went out to save you! And I almost got killed! Now I find out that you weren't even being held prisoner! That you're working for them! That somehow … you were trying to use me! Now, if you don't think I deserve an explanation, I seriously hope that you can swim, because I'm liable to throw you right off this balcony!"

Julia stared at him in silence.

"You … you wouldn't!" she said, after a moment. "I … I'd hit the beach!"

Daniel moved closer to her, staring into her eyes, "Even better!" he said. "Now, are you going to talk? Or shall we try?"

Julia glanced down, then reluctantly, she nodded.

"Okay. I … I'm an undercover agent, working for the government."

Daniel stared at her for a moment, then he leaned back and laughed.

"Ha, ha, ha. You seriously expect me to believe that?" he asked.

Julia shot him a look.

"It's true! I … I infiltrated the organization. My mission was to find out all about them. It's an organization called Spider."

"Spider?" Daniel repeated, remembering what Marshall had told him about what they had found on John Keaton's computer.

"They … they call themselves Spider because they say they have a web which stretches everywhere."

"And who are 'they'?"

"Businessmen mostly, powerful men, rich, immensely rich. Recently, they've been working on some kind of undercover operation, top secret. I couldn't get closer to it. All I know is that it involves finding a young Chinese girl."

"Suzie Q," Daniel said.

"Yes … yes, Suzie Q, that's what you called her.'

"What 'I' called her?" Daniel asked, staring at her.

Julia nodded, "Yes," she said. "We … that is … the organization, moni-
tored a conversation between you and Keaton before they picked you
both up."

Daniel gazed down thoughtfully, trying to remember.

"What do they want with her?" he asked after a moment's silence.

"I … I don't know. It … it's something to do with a butterfly, whatever
that means."

"A butterfly?" Daniel repeated, remembering what Heller had told him.

He stared thoughtfully down again, then looked back up at her.

"That night, you didn't just happen by, did you?" he said. "And later,
when you saved me from those men, you were following me."

Julia nodded, "Yes. They … they had you prisoner. Apparently they
were trying to find out what you knew about where Suzie Q is. I … I
don't know who they were, they weren't part of Spider."

"They're another interested party," Daniel said. "Go on, what happened
before that? Apparently, you were present when Keaton was being
tortured."

Julia glanced quickly down, "Ye … yes! It … it was horrible! Poor Mr.
Keaton, he … he didn't know where the girl was."

"But I did?" Daniel asked.

Julia nodded, still glancing down, "Yes, yes, you did. They had you prisoner too. At first, they beat you but you wouldn't talk, then someone must have hit you on the head too hard because when you came to, you couldn't remember anything. Of course, they didn't believe you, so the beating continued. They were going to torture you too, but I convinced them that you were telling the truth, that you had really lost your memory and that they wouldn't learn anything through torture, so I came up with a plan. They were to dump you where you'd left your car and I was to find you and get close to you. You hadn't seen me when they were beating you, so you didn't know me. I convinced them that you'd open up with someone who got close to you, that it would help you to remember."

"But I rejected you," Daniel said with a grin.

Julia nodded.

"Plan B was that I would get captured and that you'd desperately try to remember where the girl was and what had happened so that you could save me."

"But that didn't work either," Daniel said.

Julia glanced down and shook her head, "They decided that the first course of action was best, to torture you."

"Nice!" Daniel said, turning to glance down towards the ocean.

"You … still don't remember, do you?"

Daniel continued to gaze down at the waves crashing up onto the beach below.

He shook his head, "I don't remember a thing," he said. "Except … a blinding light …"

"Yes," Julia said. "They put a spotlight on you when they were asking you questions and beating you. I … I thought that they were either going to beat you to death … or … or torture you to death."

Daniel looked at her.

"Don't tell me you care," he said.

"Of course I care!" Julia said indignantly. "I'm not one of them! I'm a government agent!"

"So, what about Keaton?" Daniel asked.

"I … I couldn't stop them," Julia said, glancing down. "They tortured him when you were still unconscious. They knew you had a meeting with him, they thought you had told him where the girl was. Apparently, Keaton tried to leave the organization, so they grew suspicious. They began following him, they listened in on his calls. When he contacted you, they began to follow you too. They were sure that he knew something, that he was going to find out, where the Chinese girl was."

"So, your job was to help them find the girl? That's great of you! And what if they kill her when they find her? Have you thought about that?"

Julia looked back up at him, "I … I would try to protect her!" she said. "Look," she continued, "we don't know why Spider wants her, why she is so important to them and what they're planning. As soon as they have her, I'll be in a position to find out and pass on the information."

"At the risk of a girl's life?" Daniel said, staring at her.

Julia hesitated looking at him, then she nodded, "It's a chance I have to take," she said. She leaned closer to him, staring into his eyes. "Don't you see? We have to find out what Spider is panning! Other lives may be at risk!"

Daniel stared back at her, then glanced down.

"Can you try?" Julia said. "Try to remember?"

Daniel shook his head, "I don't remember a thing," he said.

"I ... I got hold of any information I could on you," Julia said. "I thought it might help."

"The orphanage?" Daniel said, glancing back up at her. "My boxing career? The police? The bribe scandal?"

Julia nodded, "I went through all of it. Is it true? They really called you The Black Cat?"

Daniel nodded. He smiled to himself, remembering.

"I grew up in an orphanage," he said. "I never knew who my parents were. I was bullied every day, bullied and sometimes tortured. I vowed that it wouldn't happen anymore, so I ran away and learned to fight. I started wearing black, I don't know why, to shock people I guess, or maybe ... I felt that some part of me had already died. I got a small reputation as a fighter. They called me The Black Cat because they said I moved fast and healed quickly, and also because I always wore black. I was angry, angry at the world. Then, one day, I'd had enough of beating people. I decided to turn to helping people instead, so I joined the police."

"And that's when …"

"There was a bribery allegation. No proof, no evidence, that's because I was innocent. So I left."

Julia gazed at him for a long moment.

"If you always wear black, why is it you drive a bright yellow car?"

Daniel grinned, "I wear black because I got used to wearing black, it's a habit I guess. As for the car, well, I got a good deal on it!"

Julia laughed.

"A Volkswagen Beetle? Isn't it kind of slow?"

"Mine's got a modified engine," Daniel said. "I got a good deal on that too."

"Did you … did you ever get over your being angry at the world?"

Daniel stared at her, for a long moment, then shook his head, "No. No, I never did," he said finally.

CHAPTER 20

Julia sat on the sofa with a drink that Daniel had poured for her in her hand. She glanced down at the mess that was still on the floor.

"Are you really going to fire your cleaning lady?" she asked.

Daniel sipped his drink, then shook his head, "No, I don't even have a cleaning lady," he said.

Julia grinned.

They both sat in silence for a few moments, then Julia spoke.

"Daniel," she said, looking at him.

Daniel turned to her.

"Is there anything ... anything at all that could make you remember?"

Daniel gazed down at his drink, then shook his head, "I've tried," he said. "I can't remember a thing, apart from that blinding white light."

Julia sighed, "There must be something, some way to make you remember."

Daniel closed his eyes and tried to think back, but all he got was a blank space filled with light.

He shook his head again.

"Nothing," he said.

"What about the Chinese woman?" Julia asked. "The Chinese woman named Lin?"

Daniel shook his head again, "I don't know any Chinese woman called Lin," he said. "At least, as far as I know."

Julia studied him for a moment, then spoke again, "I called the orphanage trying to find out about you. Apparently a Chinese woman used to go there asking about you, wanting to know how you were, if you were safe."

Daniel turned and studied her, his eyes widening, "You're joking!" he said.

Julia looked at him, seeing the surprised expression on his face.

"You didn't know?" she asked.

Daniel stared at her in amazement.

"How ... how could I have?" he said.

He glanced down thoughtfully.

"Damn it!" he said. "Who the hell was that woman?"

"I guess … she might be connected with Suzie Q," Julia said.

Daniel stood up and started to pace up and down the room.

"Who the hell was she?" he said to himself again, staring down at the floor. "Why did she ask about me"

Julia shrugged, "We don't know. She seems to be missing too."

Julia thought for a moment.

"Daniel," she said. "Is there … is there some place safe where you'd hide someone? If someone were looking for them?"

Daniel stopped pacing and looked down at her.

"Somewhere safe … ?"

"Yes," Julia said. "Where would you hide someone."

Daniel put his hand to his head trying to think.

"I … I have no idea … I …"

Julia sighed, watching as Daniel stood in the centre of the room trying to remember. After a moment, she turned and glanced down once more at the mess on the floor. Suddenly, she noticed the photo of a girl in her twenties with long auburn hair.

"Who's that?" she asked, pointing down at the photo.

Daniel stepped over to where she was pointing and looked down at the photo.

"That …" he sighed. "That's my ex-wife. We were together for about two years. One day, she just … just walked out on me."

Julia looked up at him, "I … I'm sorry," she said.

Suddenly, Daniel remembered something. Slowly, he knelt down and picked up the photo.

"What is it?" Julia asked, watching him closely.

"Her father, he has a cabin up in the mountains, just outside the city."

Julia studied him thoughtfully, "And you think …?"

Daniel turned to her.

"If I was going to hide someone," he said, "that's where I'd hide them."

CHAPTER 21

Morning was breaking as they drove through the suburbs heading out of the city.

"So, why'd you choose this city?" Julia asked. "I mean, when you ran away from the orphanage?"

Daniel stared at the road in front of him. The road was completely deserted. It was still too early even for early morning traffic.

"The orphanage was inland," Daniel said. "On one side, the desert, and on the other side, flat grassland. I just continued heading west. I didn't stop until I hit the ocean. That's why I call it Ocean City. With a boat on the ocean, you have the feeling that you could escape, go anywhere you want in the world, feel completely free. Also I like the mountains and the forests nearby. I decided that this is where I would make my home. I was lucky to be able to buy a place near the beach, just in front of the ocean. It's the only lucky break in my life."

Julia glanced at him, then she gently squeezed his shoulder, "You deserve happiness Daniel," she said.

He glanced at her quickly, then back at the road.

"Thank you," he said softly. "But I guess … there are a lot of people out there who deserve happiness. Good, decent people."

Julia studied him, "That doesn't sound like an angry Daniel speaking," she said.

Daniel shrugged, "I have my moments," he said.

Julia studied his face, he was unshaven, his face was beaten and bruised, and he looked tired, but there was something about him, something that she couldn't put into words.

"Thank you for coming to save me," she said softly.

Daniel merely nodded slightly, as if he were embarrassed at her words, and continued driving along the road towards the mountains.

After a moment, he put on the radio.

Oh, I like this song!" Julia said, as a song began to play over the radio.

"Really? What is it?" Daniel asked, keeping his eyes on the road.

"It's called 'Brave' by Jhene Aiko"

"Never heard of it," Daniel said.

Julia looked at him, then smiled. She touched his shoulder again and gently squeezed it, then leaned back to listen to the words of the song as

Daniel drove towards the mountains rising up in front of them further along the road.

*

Sometime later, they were driving up a mountain dirt-track road which weaved its way through a forest of tall pine trees.

"It's just up ahead," Daniel said.

Julia took out the gun that Daniel had given her and checked it.

"What are you doing?" Daniel asked.

Julia looked at him.

"Just taking precautions," she said. "Just in case."

"Yeah, well, just keep the gun out of sight, okay? It was the one thing my ex-wife got very nervous about."

Julia smiled, "Don't worry, I'm not going to shoot her."

She tucked the gun into her jeans behind her and pulled her red-check shirt down over it. The dirt-track road wound to the left and Daniel drove along it slowly following it round until it straightened out and exited the forest entering a clearing just up ahead. He stopped the car on the edge of the clearing, staring across at what was on the other side. Julia saw an old log cabin on the far side of the clearing with a car parked outside it.

"Nice place," she said, as Daniel started the car forward again heading across the clearing towards the cabin. Julia glanced to the left and saw a small stream running down a slope not far from the cabin on the other side of the clearing. Someone was sitting nearby it. The person stood up as they drove closer and Julia saw that it was an auburn-haired girl in her twenties. The girl was now standing facing them, watching as the car came across the clearing towards the cabin. As they neared her, Julia recognized her face from the photograph on the floor of Daniel's apartment. The door of the cabin suddenly opened and two people stepped out looking towards the approaching car. Daniel saw that both the woman and the young girl, who were now standing outside the door, were oriental.

Daniel grinned, "We've found them!" he said.

Julia glanced at him and smiled, "Well done!" she said.

Daniel stopped his car beside the other car which was parked just beside the cabin. Both he and Julia quickly got out. The Chinese woman seemed to smile at him, and the young Chinese girl who Daniel imagined to be about sixteen years old and was dressed in a dark school uniform, suddenly ran towards him and threw her arms around him, hugging him tightly.

"You're back! You're back!" the girl shouted happily. "I knew you wouldn't leave us! I knew you wouldn't leave us!"

Daniel glanced over at Julia with a surprised look on his face.

The girl with the auburn hair, who'd been sitting beside the stream, marched over towards them. Daniel looked at his ex-wife marching towards him, and noticed that she had an angry look on her face.

"Carole …" he began to say.

"Where the hell have you been?" his ex-wife, Carole, shouted before he could utter another word.

She stopped just a few feet in front of him staring angrily into his eyes.

Suddenly, she noticed the bruises and cuts marking his face.

"What the hell happened to you?" she asked, gazing at him.

"It's a long story," Daniel said.

He pushed the young girl away from him and looked down at her sweet innocent looking face.

"You're Suzie Q I take it," he said.

The young Chinese girl looked up at him strangely, "You … you don't know who I am?" she asked.

Daniel smiled down at her, "I … I've had some problems remembering things recently."

Carole looked at Julia, observing her up and down with a distasteful look on her face.

"Who's this?" she asked, pointing at Julia.

"She's a friend,' Daniel said.

Julia held out her hand to Carole with a smile.

"My name's Julia," she said.

Carole merely stared at her with an angry looking expression.

Daniel looked towards the Chinese woman who was still standing by the door of the cabin observing him.

"I have to talk to her,' he said, gesturing towards the woman.

He took a step to move past Carole but she quickly grabbed his arm.

"Oh no you don't!" she said. "You and me are going to have a discussion right now!"

Daniel took her hand off his arm, stared at her for a moment, then strode past her towards the cabin. The Chinese woman remained still, waiting as he walked towards her.

"Who are you?" Daniel asked as he stopped in front of her.

The Chinese woman gazed carefully into his eyes before answering.

"You … do not remember what I told you just a few days ago?" she asked.

Daniel gazed back at her, then shook his head.

"No, I … I had an accident. I've forgotten everything about the last few days."

The woman smiled at him, then moved forward and gently laid a hand on his shoulder.

"Daniel …" she said tenderly.

He saw the tears which were now forming in her eyes.

"Who are you?" he asked again. "Who … who am I?" he added.

The woman hesitated before speaking, still gazing into his eyes. Daniel saw a tear run down her cheek.

"I … I'm …" she started to say.

Then a sound suddenly made her look up.

Daniel quickly glanced round.

He saw the helicopter coming towards them across the clearing and stared up at it with a look of shock on his face, then he shouted for everyone to run for cover.

CHAPTER 22

They ran for the cars. A sudden burst of machine-gun fire sounded and bullets churned up the ground just in front of the cabin, then the helicopter turned and more machine-gun fire sounded, this time spitting bullets into the metal and glass of the car behind which Daniel had leapt. Both Julia and Carole dove to the ground rolling and crawling towards the shelter of the car as bullets dug into the earth all around them. Suzie Q screamed falling to her knees and placing her hands over her ears trying to cut out the noise of the chattering machine-gun. Daniel leapt out from behind the car, rolled and aimed his gun up at the hovering helicopter. He fired shot after shot in rapid fire then saw the helicopter veer to the right as one of his bullets hit the pilot. The man by the open door of the helicopter on the machine-gun fell out with a loud yell and then the helicopter veered completely out of control heading across the clearing towards the tall pines of the surrounding forest. Daniel watched as it sped towards the trees surrounding the clearing and then crashed into them with a loud explosion that spat out fire and metal and glass as a cloud of smoke now began to rise up from the flames. Daniel got up onto his feet watching the various debris and the main bulk of the helicopter fall down onto the clearing amidst the rising flames.

"Mama! Mama!" he heard someone cry out from behind.

Daniel spun round and saw the Chinese woman lying on the ground in a pool of blood. Suzie, the young Chinese girl, ran over to her and knelt down by her side crying hysterically. He saw both Carole and Julia get up off the ground from behind a car and looking over at Suzie who was now kneeling down and hugging her mother and crying and calling out "Mama! Mama!" incessantly.

Daniel ran over to her and knelt down beside her. He took Suzie in his arms and held her tightly.

"Mama! Mama!" Suzie continued to cry out as she shook with tears running down her face, staring down at her mother's lifeless and bloody body.

Daniel didn't know what to say to the girl to console her, so he merely held her in his arms as tightly as he could rocking her backward and forward.

Suddenly, another sound came across the sky towards them. Daniel quickly glanced round and saw another helicopter flying towards them.

"Into the car! Quickly!" he shouted.

He had no need to tell both Carole and Julia which car he meant, for the car which had been parked when both he and Julia had arrived had been riddled with bullets and was possibly out of service. Both Carole and Julia quickly jumped into Daniel's yellow Volkswagen as Daniel had to forcibly drag Suzie away from her mother's dead body. Daniel pulled Suzie over to his car, pushed her inside, then jumped in behind the steering wheel. He started the engine and spun the car around, kicking up earth from the wheels as he went. The machine-gunner on the approaching helicopter began to fire down at them. A rain of bullets spat down towards them as Daniel gunned the car as fast as it would go across the clearing towards the cover of the trees and the dirt-track road on the far side. He lowered the window as he drove and fired up at the helicopter. His car hit a bump in the clearing and Daniel almost dropped his gun as the car seemed to fly across the ground and land with a sickening thud, its wheels spinning fast, forcing the car forward and on towards the trees as the chatter of the machine-gun fire from above almost drowned out the sound of the car's engine. Suddenly, the car reached the trees and was about to speed along the forest dirt-track when bullets fired from the helicopter hit a back tyre causing Daniel to momentarily lose control. The car spun on the dirt-track narrowly missing a tree and came to a stop.

"Everybody out!" Daniel shouted.

He grabbed Suzie's hand, pulled her over to his side of the car and dragged her out as she screamed and fell out of the car through the open door. More bullets rained down around them as the chatter of machine-gun fire sounded again from the helicopter which had now descended from the sky to just a few yards from the ground in front of the first tall pines that lined the clearing. Bullets spat past the trees and along the dirt-track hitting

Daniel's car as both Carole and Julia ran in separate directions trying to find cover behind trees and in the surrounding bushes. Daniel, who had dragged the screaming Suzie over behind a tree, heard another scream and looked back. He saw Carole falling as if in slow motion towards the ground. Blood spurted out of her back as she fell, her eyes were open wide as was her mouth, which was also gaping open as a piercing scream escaped her.

"Carol!" Daniel cried out, unconsciously letting go of Suzie's hand as he ran back over towards the girl he'd once loved and still loved in his heart. Bullets rained around him, but he was completely oblivious to the danger as he ran over to Carole's falling body. He reached her, not aware if the machine-gun was still firing or not as he knelt down beside her and lifted her body, holding her so that he could look into her face. Carole stared up at him, her eyes flickering as blood ran down from her mouth.

"Carole!" he cried. "Carole!"

"D … Daniel …" she managed to say.

She tried to raise her hand to his face, then her hand fell down beside her body and her eyes glassed over. She now stared up at him, still and completely lifeless.

"Carole! Carole! Carole!" Daniel shouted, shaking her as if he were trying to bring her back to life.

He stared down at her face, then squeezed his eyes tightly shut and pulled her towards him, holding her tightly in his arms.

"Aaaaargh!"

The sudden scream came from behind him making him turn. He was just in time to see two men dragging Suzie over to the helicopter which had now landed in the clearing just beyond the trees. A fierce animal-like snarl now began to distort his face. He jumped up, his gun in his hand, and ran back towards the clearing and the helicopter. The men pushed Suzie on board and got into the helicopter behind her just as

Daniel reached the clearing. He raised his gun to fire at the helicopter which was now just beginning to take off.

"Noooo!" Daniel shouted, aiming his gun up at the helicopter.

"Daniel no!"

Julia came running out from behind the trees knocking his arm down and spoiling his aim as he fired, his bullet now hitting the ground in front of him.

"You might hit the girl!" she shouted to him.

Daniel turned to look at her, his face filled with anger as his eyes burned into hers. The helicopter rose up further off the ground and now veered quickly away to the left climbing in the sky as it went. Daniel glanced back up at it, his mouth tightly pulled back over his clenched teeth as he watched it go. He stood for a moment in silence breathing heavily, then he turned suddenly and aimed his gun towards Julia who had blood running down the side of her face.

"Daniel … wha …?' Julia said, staring wide-eyed at the gun aimed towards her.

"You!" Daniel said, spitting out the word angrily as he spoke. "You brought them here!"

Julia stared at the gun in Daniel's hand with widening fearful eyes, not knowing what to say.

CHAPTER 23

Julia raised her hands in a defensive gesture. She shook her head.

"Daniel ... you ... you've got this wrong. I ... I'm not responsible for this ... Daniel ... you've got to believe me!"

"Drop the gun!" Daniel shouted.

Julia hesitated, then let go of her gun.

"Kick it over here!" Daniel said.

"Daniel ... look ..."

"Kick the goddamn gun over here!" Daniel shouted.

Julia kicked the gun over to him.

"Daniel ... I ... I know you must find it hard to trust me right now, but you ... you have to believe me ..."

"What did they give you?" Daniel asked. "A special device? An electronic bug? So that they could follow us when I brought you here?"

Julia shook her head, "Look … Daniel, you … you have this all wrong! I … I don't have anything, no bugs! The only thing I can think of is that … they put a bug on your car. Do you have GPS?"

Daniel shook his head, "I've never had GPS on my car!"

"Then … then they may have bugged it!" Julia said desperately.

"No," Daniel said, shaking his head. "It's you! I know it's you! Take off your clothes!"

Julia stared at him.

"What?" she asked.

"I said take off your clothes! I want to check to see if you're wearing some device!"

"Look … I … I'm not wearing any device!"

"Take them off! Now!" Daniel shouted, moving closer and aiming his gun directly at her head.

Julia stared at the gun. She took a deep breath, then began to undo her shirt. Daniel watched, his eyes blazing angrily, ready to fire at any second if Julia made any false moves. Julia took off her shirt. She hesitated, staring at the gun, then next took off her jeans. Daniel stared at her as she stood in front of him in her undclothes.

"Everything!" Daniel said.

"Hey, look …"

"I said everything!" Daniel shouted.

Julia hesitated again, still staring at the gun, then she took off her bra and stopped.

"I said … everything!" Daniel shouted again, pointing his gun down towards her panties.

Julia hesitated once more, then tucked her thumbs into her panties and slid them down over her legs. As she stood up straight she covered her body with her hands.

"Hands on the head!" Daniel shouted. "Feet apart! Wide! I don't want you running off!"

Julia hesitated again, then complied, her face blushing as she now stood completely naked in front of him.

"Now back up!" Daniel said.

Slowly, Julia backed away.

Daniel moved forward and bent down to look through Julia's clothes.

"I … I tell you, I wasn't carrying anything!" Julia said, watching Daniel.

Daniel looked through all of her clothes and found nothing, then he stood up and gazed at her body up and down.

"Turn around!" he said.

Julia breathed heavily staring at him, then let out a long sigh and turned around.

She heard him move closer behind her as he checked to make sure that she wasn't wearing a bug

"Okay,' he said. "You can put your arms down and turn around."

Julia lowered her arms and turned to face him, her face feeling hot from the shame and the deeply embarrassed blush that she knew she had.

"Satisfied?" she said bitterly, staring into his eyes.

Daniel pointed down to her clothes, "You can get dressed," he said.

Suddenly, Julia raised her hand and slapped him hard across the face.

Daniel touched the sting on his face gingerly.

"I really hope you're satisfied!" Julia shouted angrily.

Daniel shook his head, "No," he said, staring back at her. "I'm not!'

Julia abruptly walked past him to her clothes which lay on the ground and began to get dressed.

"Either there's a tracking device on you, or it's on your car!" Julia said, staring back at him bitterly. "Go check!"

Daniel watched her getting dressed for a moment, then glanced back along the dirt-track towards his car. The car stood crosswise across the track. He looked at the bullet holes across its side wondering if it would still work, then he walked over to it trying not to glance down at Carole's body as he went. When he reached it, he bent down and looked underneath. At first, he saw nothing, then he noticed a small device which had been attached underneath near the back of the car. He reached towards it and pulled it off, then stood up looking at it.

"I didn't know about it," Julia said from behind him. "Believe me."

Daniel turned and glanced at her, then he threw the device down on the ground and stepped on it hard, crushing it.

He stared down at it for a moment, the looked back up at her "Sorry," he said to her.

Julia glanced down at Carole's dead body lying just a few feet away, "I … I'm sorry too," she said sadly.

Suddenly, two cars sounded speeding along the dirt-track towards them. Both Daniel and Julia spun round as the cars skidded to a stop just a few yards from them. The cars' doors opened and at least eight men got out of both cars. All of the men were Chinese.

CHAPTER 24

The room was semi-dark.

Both Daniel and Julia sat opposite each other at a long table which resembled a table used for board room meetings. There were no windows. As far as Daniel could work out, once they had returned to the city they had been taken down to some secret underground room. Daniel leaned back in the comfortable black leather chair, the chair creaking in the silence of the room as he did so, and sipped some water from the glass he had been given. Daniel gazed across the table at Julia. She seemed nervous, her eyes darting left and right, looking around the room. Suddenly, she looked at him and leaned forward.

"What do you think they want?" she asked.

Daniel studied her for a moment in silence. He placed the glass of water back down onto the table and stared back into her eyes.

"You tell me," he said. "I think there's something you're not telling me, right? I mean, if you really work for a government agency, where are all your people? And don't tell me that you prefer to work alone."

Julia avoided Daniel's stare and looked down at the highly polished table. She hesitated, then she spoke.

"I'm ... I'm what's known as a rogue agent," she said.

Daniel raised his eyebrows, "A rogue agent?" he repeated.

Julia nodded, "Yes. I was given an assignment, me alone, to infiltrate the organization known as Spider."

"With no back up?"

Julia shook her head and leaning closer to him across the table, "Spider is a large organization with a growing number of people, people in power. We believe that my agency has been compromised. Only two people know that I'm not really rogue and I report directly to them."

"So ... no back up," Daniel said, staring across at her.

Julia shook her head again, "No back up," she confirmed.

"So ... if your organization's been compromised, how did they know to trust you?"

A smile came onto to Julia's lips, "Because I'm trustworthy," she said.

"So say you," Daniel said, still staring at her intensely.

"Only two people know about me," Julia said. "They trust me more than anyone else, that's why they gave me the mission."

Daniel took another sip of his drink and sat back thinking about what Julia had said.

"When was the last time you made your report?" he asked.

"The last night that I saw you, before I supposedly disappeared."

"Trying to make me remember out of desperation to save your life."

"That's right."

"So ... you didn't notify your mysterious boss about Carole's mountain cabin?"

"No. That didn't come from me ... look, I told you, we're on the same side."

Daniel stared at her coldly for a moment, then shrugged, "Sorry, but at this precise moment, I don't trust anyone."

"Look, why don't you just ... just leave all this! They've got the girl, that's what they wanted ... if we get out of ..." she gestured around the secret underground room, "... this, you can just walk away. It's not your problem anymore."

There was a stilled silence in the room as Daniel stared back into her eyes. Julia leaned back from the table seeing an anger begin to grow in Daniel's expression. His eyes now seemed even colder than before. Whereas before Daniel had seemed calm in spite of his cold stare, Julia now witnessed an intense fury building up inside him. Suddenly, he leaned forward and slammed his fist down hard onto the table making both the table and Julia jump together.

"Walk away?" Daniel shouted. "I just saw the person I love get gunned down right in front of me! Another young girl I can't remember confides her trust in me and is taken for God knows what! Her mother, a woman who knew probably knew where I came from, was gunned down in front of her eyes! And you just want me to walk away?"

Daniel's voice had risen so loudly that someone outside the room had obviously heard him. The door to the room opened and both Daniel and Julia looked round. The big Chinese guard, Daniel recognized as Yak, came into the room and stood to the side looking down at them both in silence. Behind him, Wang came into the room wearing a very smart, expensive looking suit. He stopped as he entered and gazed down at them.

"About time!" Daniel said, glaring angrily across at him.

"I see you're getting bored," Wang said, sitting down in a chair at the head of the table nearby the open door. "You're conversation was very ... illuminating."

He sat looking at them both.

Daniel glanced up at the camera on the wall near the ceiling. He smiled, "Don't you have anything better to watch?" he asked. "What's the matter? Run out of Jackie Chan cartoons?"

Wang stared at him, "I find your humour, under the circumstances, most amusing McGlade. However, I'm not in the mood for jokes at the moment. It seems we have both ..." he paused, glancing down sadly, "... we have both lost someone we loved."

Both Daniel and Julia stared at him, surprised to see the grief shown on his face.

"Suzie Q's mother?" Daniel asked softly.

Wang nodded, still gazing down at the table, then he pulled out a photograph from his inside jacket pocket and slid it across the table-top to them. Both Daniel and Julia glanced down at the photograph. Daniel reached out and turned it towards him so that he could study the face of Suzie Q's mother carefully.

"Who ... who was she?" Daniel asked, still studying the photograph carefully.

Wang paused before answering. The silence in the room had a palpable feel to it.

"She was my sister," Wang said finally.

Daniel looked at him and saw that he was trying to fight back the tears that were coming into his eyes.

CHAPTER 25

"So, that means that Suzie Q is …" Daniel began to say.

"Is my niece," Wang said. "Her name is Suzie Qi."

Daniel hesitated before asking his next question, "Why do they want her?" he asked.

Wang shook his head, "I don't know. My sister contacted me by phone. It was a quick conversation. She said that she and my niece had entered the country and were somewhere safe, with someone who was looking after them. I imagine she meant you. She said that there were people after them, that they couldn't come to me because the people knew they were my family, that I'd be watched. A few days later, you came to me and asked me where my niece was, where my sister was, saying that you had lost your memory. I … I didn't understand what was happening, so I had you followed."

"And that's how your men found the cabin?" Daniel asked.

Wang nodded, "My men informed me that you were leaving the city, I guessed it was to see my sister and my niece, so I sent more men after you."

"To protect us," Daniel said, staring at Wang thoughtfully.

"To protect my sister and my niece," Wang said. "Unfortunately …" Wang glanced down again, " … they arrived too late." He paused, then looked back up at Daniel, "You really did lose your memory, didn't you?" he asked.

Daniel nodded, then looked across at Julia, "Someone told me I'd been hit over the head too hard."

Julia glanced away from his eyes.

"Any … any idea where she's been taken?" Julia asked, now looking at Wang.

Wang breathed deeply, then nodded, "My men were able to follow the helicopter flight. Apparently, my niece had been taken to a private airfield. There, she was put onto a private jet."

Daniel leaned forward, "To where?" he asked.

Wang looked at him, "Going to Hong Kong," he said. "They're taking her back."

"Hong Kong!" Daniel repeated, shaking his head.

"And, apparently, one of your friends is on the plane with them," Wang added.

Daniel looked up, he stared across at Wang.

"Who?" he asked.

"Inspector Marshall Tiloni," Wang replied. "He is a friend of yours, is he not?"

Daniel stared back at him with a shocked look on his face. Slowly, he leaned back in his chair, the chair creaking in the silence as he stared blankly in front of him as if deep in thought.

*

"What is this place?" Daniel asked, as they walked through the corridor outside the room leading to a staircase.

"Underground offices," Wang said, glancing back at him as they walked.

"You're not just a restaurant owner, are you?" Daniel asked.

Julia, who was walking beside Daniel, glanced at him, "You finally worked that out?" she asked.

Daniel gave her a look.

"So …" Daniel continued, looking back at Wang as they reached the staircase and started going up, "…what are you into? Drugs? Smuggling? Weapons?"

Wang stopped on the steps of the staircase and turned to look back at him.

"I'm into information, McGlade, information."

He turned and started up the staircase again. Daniel glanced at Julia, then continued up the staircase behind him. When they reached the top, they exited through a secret door which led out into the kitchen of Wang's restaurant.

"So, all of this is a front," Daniel said, glancing around at the Chinese cooks and the other kitchen staff busily working in the kitchen.

Wang said nothing as they walked through the kitchen and exited through the door leading to the large restaurant room. Chang, who was standing to one side, nodded at Wang as Wang led them over to the restaurant door and then held it open for them.

"Your car's outside McGlade," Wang said. "The wheels have been changed, but the bullet holes in the body of the car remain. You have a choice, you can either follow us to an airfield and fly to Hong Kong, or you can merely turn away and forget this whole affair."

"Even with what I now know about you?" Daniel asked, looking at him in surprise.

"I trust you will not go to the police," Wang said. He glanced at Julia, "I daresay you will want to come with us," he said to her.

Julia nodded, "Yes, yes, I do. I have to finish this."

Daniel glanced at her, then walked out into the street towards his car. The yellow VW Beetle looked even more beat up than usual with a line of bullet holes going across its side. Daniel stood looking at it.

A young man, who was passing by in the street, suddenly stopped to look at the bullet holes in the car's side.

"Hey! Neat!" he said. "Neat decoration!"

He placed his hands in front of him, studying the bullet holes as if he were framing the image of the car, "But … I think it would have been much better if you'd had the holes designed to go up a little more to the right, just a little more, it would have looked more artistic, you know?"

Daniel looked at the young man for a moment.

"Right," Daniel said. "You're right. I'll remember to point that out to the next person who's trying to kill me."

The young man's foolish grin disappeared and his jaw dropped as he stared back at Daniel with a look of both shock and surprise on his face.

Daniel glanced at Julia, "Are you getting in? We've got a place where we have to be!"

A smile etched itself onto Julia's face, then she nodded and stepped towards the car.

The young man stood on the pavement watching, as two black cars led the way along the street followed by the bullet-ridden yellow VW Beetle behind them.

CHAPTER 26

Daniel leaned forward and looked out of the plane's small window. It was dark outside, but as he glanced down, he saw the coloured lights of the tall towers in Hong Kong. He stared down at the city with a feeling that he was entering another world.

"See anything?" Julia asked, sitting beside him.

Daniel leaned back and gestured for her to lean across him and look out of the window. She leaned across and gazed down at the city below.

"Hong Kong," she said softly to herself. "It looks so different from up here."

"Been here before?" Daniel asked her.

Julia nodded, "Once. A person could get lost down there, literally."

"Then I'll try not to lose you," Daniel said.

Julia leaned back and smiled at him, "Promise?" she asked.

Daniel gazed at her for a moment, then nodded, "Promise," he said.

*

Two black sedan-looking cars were waiting for them at the airport. Wang and Yak, his large bodyguard, and three other of his men, got into the first car, while Daniel, Julia and two more of Wang's men got into the car behind. Daniel looked out of the window as they rode from the airport and into Hong Kong city. He gazed at the Hong Kong streets, surprised to see so many neon coloured lights on the buildings showing Chinese symbols and signs. The cars finally stopped outside a medium-sized hotel down near the Hong Kong bay area. They went inside following behind Wang and his men who waited, hanging around the hotel's lobby, while Wang went over to the reception to see about the rooms. Daniel glanced at the hotel's interior design and declined politely when a young Chinese girl came over offering the new guests a free welcoming drink on a tray.

Julia observed the girl as she walked away, "Cute, isn't she?" she asked, glancing at Daniel.

Daniel shrugged, "Not really my type," he said.

"No?' Julia said, now observing him. "So, what is your type?" she asked with a smile.

Daniel shot her a glance, "You know my type. She's lying dead outside a cabin on a mountainside!" he said abruptly.

Julia glanced down, "I … I'm sorry," she said. "I … I didn't mean to …"

Wang came over to them followed by his men and handed them the keys to their hotel room.

"Get some rest," he said. "I have contacts in this city, my men will find out where my niece has been taken. Maybe by morning we will know."

He studied Daniel for a moment.

"Are you still sure you want to help?"

"Nothing could stop me,' Daniel answered, staring back into Wang's eyes.

Wang nodded, "Good. Get some rest, both of you."

He turned and walked back across the hotel lobby with his men, talking to them in Chinese.

Daniel looked down at the room's key number he'd been given.

"Looks like we'll be sharing a room," he said.

"Does that disturb you?" Julia asked.

Daniel shrugged, "Not at all. If there's only one bed, I'll sleep on the sofa," he said. "If they have one," he added.

                    *

The room was spacious with a large double bed and a wide ceiling to floor window with a sliding door which opened out onto a balcony overlooking the Hong Kong bay area. There was no sofa. As Julia tried the bed, Daniel stepped out onto the balcony and stood gazing down at the neon lights of the busy city beneath him.

After a few moments, he felt the presence of Julia beside him.

"Beautiful, isn't it?" she said, gazing down at the city below.

Daniel said nothing, he merely stared down at the city as if lost in thought.

Suddenly, Julia turned to him.

"Why did she leave you?" she asked.

Daniel remained silent, staring down for a long moment, then he shrugged.

"Maybe she felt I wasn't worth it," he said. "I … I tried to make the relationship work, but … basically, I'm no one. I'm from nowhere. Maybe she was right, I didn't deserve her. Maybe … maybe I don't deserve anyone."

Julia studied him.

"Is … is that why you have a death wish?" she asked.

Daniel quickly glanced at her.

Julia shrugged, "My guess is that she couldn't stand seeing you get beaten up … get almost killed … my guess is that she really loved you."

Daniel stared at her.

Julia gazed back at him, wondering if she was right to speak her mind. She was sure that the anger she'd seen burst inside him in Wang's secret underground room was going to burst again, but this time, Daniel seemed to control it. He glanced back down at the city, then shook his head, "I didn't deserve her," he said, his voice almost a whisper as he spoke. "She could do …" he paused, glancing down, then corrected himself before continuing, "… could have done … better than me," he said, finishing his sentence.

Julia reached forward with her hand and touched his arm gently.

"That's not true," she said. "You … you are worth someone's love … you were worthy of her love."

Daniel stood in silence, then shook his head, "I've never been worthy of anyone's love," he said. "Especially not hers, and … I never will be."

He turned suddenly before Julia could say another word and went back into the room.

*

It was 2am when Julia leaned up from the bed and put on the bed-side lamp. She looked across at Daniel lying across the chair in what looked to be an uncomfortable position. Julia got out of bed and walked over to him. She stood gazing down at him, then picked up the blanket that had fallen onto the floor and placed it carefully back over him. She gazed down at him as he slept for a moment more, then slowly, leaned forward and gently kissed him on the head without waking him. Julia stood up and gazed down at him again in the dim light from the bed-side lamp. Tears formed in her eyes as she studied his beaten and bruised face, then suddenly, she turned and went back to bed and turned off the bed-side lamp.

*

Morning came with bright sunlight streaming through the white-lace curtains of the large balcony window. Daniel awoke to the sound of the shower coming from the bathroom. He groaned, moving stiffly in the chair, stretching his limbs which ached slightly because of his uncomfortable sleeping position. The shower stopped and a few moments later Julia appeared with a white bath-towel wrapped around her body.

She smiled as he glanced up at her.

"Good morning!" she said.

Daniel looked at her, his eyes wincing from the light streaming through the large balcony window.

"Is it?" he asked.

"Aren't you ever in a good mood?" Julia asked.

Daniel shook his head, "Nope," he answered, starting to stand up.

The room's phone rang.

Julia went over and picked it up. She listened for a moment, then answered, "Right," she said.

She looked across at Daniel as she put down the receiver.

"They've found out where they've taken Suzie,' she said.

*

The two black cars parked in a side street somewhere in Kowloon on the opposite side of the Hong Kong bay. The street's buildings looked old, almost as if they ought to have been pulled down years ago to make way for some of the modern buildings that seemed to be springing up everywhere. Wang, his bodyguard Yak, and two other of his men got out of the black car in front, while both Daniel and Julia got out of the car behind. They followed Wang and his men into one of the old buildings which looked as if it was about to fall apart, and entered a dirty looking passage-way leading to an old wooden staircase. A strange and strong smell of Chinese cooking filled the passage-way forcing Daniel to cover his nose and mouth as they started up the staircase. The rickety stair-case creaked, threatening to collapse with every foot they placed upon it. They made their way up to the fourth floor hearing an argument, a man and a woman who were shouting at each other loudly in Chinese. Daniel began to wonder just why they had come to this particular building, when they arrived on the fourth floor landing. One of Wang's men knocked at a door and the door opened slightly a few seconds later as a man peered out at them. The man seemed to hesitate, staring at them, then he opened the door wider and they walked on through into the apartment. The man who had opened the door quickly looked out to see if anybody was watching, then closed the door behind them. The apartment looked small and squalid with various objects stacked untidily up around the room between the cheap furniture. Daniel rec-ognized the two men standing patiently on either side of a middle-aged man, who was tied to a wooden chair in the centre of the room, as Wang's men. Blood was trickling down from the left corner of the man's mouth as he gazed up at Wang who now stood in front of him. Wang said something down to the man in Chinese, but the man merely glanced away and looked to the side. Wang moved forward and back-handed the man fiercely across the face as he shouted at him in Chinese again, repeating what he'd said before. The man grunted and coughed.

"Who is this?" Daniel asked, stepping forward beside Wang.

Wang turned to him, "He has a small boat in the bay. According to some contacts, he transported some men and a young girl somewhere in the early hours of the night."

"Where to?" Daniel asked.

"He won't talk," Wang said. "He's stubborn. My men offered him a large sum of money, but he still refuses to talk."

Daniel looked around at the shabby apartment, "Surprising," he said.

"It seems that money won't do it," Wang continued. "He seems to be afraid of them, seems scared stiff is what I believe you would say."

Julia moved forward, "Let me try to talk to him."

Wang raised his eyebrows looking at her, "Do you speak Chinese Miss Jones?"

Julia shook her head, "No, but you could translate."

"I'm afraid that whatever you want to say to him will be a waste of time Miss Jones. At this point, the only option open to us is torture."

Julia looked at him, "That's … what I was afraid of," she said.

Wang shrugged, "What can I say? My men tried beating him before we came here, but he still won't talk."

"So … what do you suggest?" Daniel asked.

Wang turned to him, "Pain can be very persuasive, McGlade, to even the most stubborn of men."

He turned back to his men, "Lay him on the table!"

One of Wang's men knocked everything off the top of the cheap wooden dining table near the centre of the room as two of his other men untied him from the chair and then forced him to lie down on the table top. They bound his wrists and ankles firmly to the four corners of the table then stepped back to await further orders from Wang. The man stared wide-eyed up at them, obviously worried about what they were going to do to him. Wang stepped forward, leaned down over the man and then asked him the same question again in Chinese. The man stared up at him, his eyes were afraid as he spoke quickly.

"What did he say?" Daniel asked.

Wang glanced at him, "He said they'd kill him and his family if he spoke."

"What … what are you going to do to him?" Julia asked nervously, staring down at the man.

Wang looked at her, "We have no choice," he said. "You might want to wait outside. This will be most unpleasant." He turned back to his men, "Gag him!" he said.

"Surely … there must be some other way!" Julia protested. She glanced at Daniel, "Are you okay with this?"

Daniel looked back at her, "No … no, I'm not."

He looked at Wang, "Julia's right, there must be another way."

Wang stared at him for a moment, then spoke slowly, "This man works for the organization which killed my sister … which killed your ex-wife, and which now has my niece. Who knows what they're doing to her right now? I'm sorry if you're uncomfortable with this, if you are … please leave the room."

Daniel stared back at him, then nodded and turned towards Julia, "You should go," he said.

Julia remained still, watching as one of Wang's men undid the man's belt and then pulled down his trousers. The man now lay bound to the table-top naked from the waist down. Julia studied him for a moment, then quickly glanced away.

"How are you going to do this?" Daniel asked.

Wang looked at Julia, then at Daniel, "We need the information quickly," he said. "Which part of the man's body would you say is the most sensitive?"

Daniel glanced down at the man's body in silence, almost not daring to answer the question.

Wang turned back to his men, "We'll use electricity," he said.

Yak, Wang's bodyguard, grunted, then turned and picked up a wire lying on the floor. He stripped it bare with a knife, then plugged it into the wall and came back over to the man holding two bare wires wire out towards him. The wires touched creating an electrical spark. The man stared up at the wires, his eyes opening wider in fear, then Yak reached forward and placed the two wires down against the man's body. Yak hesitated for a moment, staring down at the man, then pressed the wires together. Daniel squeezed his eyes shut as the man's body jerked uncontrollably up and down on the table and he tried to scream through the gag in his mouth as he pulled with all of his strength at the bonds holding him firmly in place. Julia turned and ran out of the room. She stood outside the door on the landing hearing the man's screams coming from inside the apartment behind her. She closed her eyes and held tightly onto the banister, then doubled over sure that she was going to be sick. The man's gargled screams behind her continued as she began to breathe heavily, her knuckles going white as she gripped the banister in front of her as tightly as possible. A few minutes went by, which for Julia seemed to be much, much longer as she listened to the man's inhuman screams, and then the screaming stopped. She was aware of somebody coming out of the apartment behind her and now standing beside her.

"He talked," Daniel said.

Julia continued to breathe heavily, then slowly, she turned to look at him.

"Was ... was that necessary?" she asked.

Daniel shrugged, "Isn't that what they did to Keaton?" he asked. "You were there."

"I … I didn't do that!" Julia said. "I tried to stop them!"

Julia turned and looked back at the apartment, then she brushed past him and went back inside. She stopped in the room and stared down at the man who was tied to the table now crying and sobbing uncontrollably. She studied his body and the wires which were now attached to him, then she doubled over again and almost retched. Wang watched her curiously as she turned and ran back out of the room. Outside on the landing, Daniel observed her as she leaned back over the banister still retching. He moved forward, then gently put an arm around her and held her tightly.

"Now I know why you were the only one in your agency who could be trusted," he said softly. "You were new, weren't you?"

Julia nodded, she turned her head and now began sobbing against Daniel's chest.

Wang came out of the apartment looking at them both.

"We know where they are," he said. "We have to go, now!"

CHAPTER 27

The small boat transported them out of the Hong Kong bay towards the open sea. Julia sat at the back of the boat watching Hong Kong city disappearing in the distance behind them. Daniel walked over to her and sat down beside her.

"Feeling better?" he asked.

Julia glanced at him, then nodded, "A little," she said.

"How'd you get involved in this business?" he asked.

Julia shrugged, "It's a long story," she said. "I guess … I just wanted to help right the wrongs of this world."

"This world can be pretty ugly, if you open your eyes to it," Daniel said.

Julia nodded, "I know. I … I thought that I could make a difference."

Daniel smiled, "A noble thought," he said.

Julia studied him, "How … how could you stay in the same room as …"

Daniel looked back at her, pausing before answering, "I've seen bad things happen before," he said.

"When … when you were, at the orphanage?" Julia asked.

Daniel glanced down, nodding, "There … and after," he said. "That's one of the reasons I ran away. In the orphanage … I didn't just witness people being tortured, I was one of the ones being tortured."

"So … that was why you learned to fight," Julia said, studying him closely.

Daniel nodded, glancing down again.

Julia touched his arm gently.

"I'm sorry," she said.

Daniel remained still for a moment, then he shrugged, looking back up at the ocean, "It was a long time ago," he said.

"But … but you still carry the bitterness inside you."

Daniel shrugged again, "I guess there are some things you can never forget. The past … can leave its scars."

"We're here!" Wang called out, turning to them from the front of the boat.

Both Daniel and Julia glanced towards him and saw that he was pointing towards an island in the distance.

"That's the island where they took her!" Wang said back to them.

*

According to the local inhabitants, the island had a small fishing village on it and had not seen many visitors until a few years ago when people from outside the small community suddenly began visiting it. The visitors didn't seem to be tourists and after a time, the people who lived on the island stopped going onto the mainland, preferring to stay on the island instead. A few fishermen who had gone to visit them from a neighbouring island were turned away coldly, saying that any visitors were now not welcome. Other fisherman from either the mainland or nearby islands had stopped going to the island altogether.

As they neared the island, the boatman, who was transporting them, pointed to a safe landing place that he knew on the other side of the island away from the small fishing village. The only other people on the boat besides the boatman were Daniel, Julia, Wang and Yak, Wang's bodyguard. Wang had told Daniel and Julia that his other men were assembling a small army of men to join them, trusted men, who were loyal to his own organization. The boatman advised them that they should hide from sight on the boat as they neared the island in case they were seen. As the boatman remained on deck, making out that he was fishing, the others hid below, checking their guns and waiting for the boat to get closer to the island. The boatman smiled, happy that he caught a few fish without even really trying, then he began to move the boat closer towards the island, approaching a beach on its far side.

He saw no sign of life as he neared the beach, and when he was close enough, he stopped the engine and let the boat drift slowly towards the shore before turning it back into the waves. A moment later, he leaned below deck and said something in Chinese.

Wang turned to Daniel and Julia, "He said we're close enough to wade ashore."

Daniel smiled as he looked at him, "Fisherman's clothes suit you," he said. "You should wear them more often."

Wang stared at him for a moment, "Funny McGlade," he said, then turned to go up on deck.

Yak, Julia and Daniel followed Wang up the steps and onto the deck and then over the side of the boat and into the water. The clear blue water came up to just over Daniel's waist as he followed the others, wading through the water towards the golden sands of the empty island beach. Palm trees hung forward from the dense green undergrowth over the quiet and empty beach as waves from the ocean lapped up onto the shore. As all four reached the beach, they turned to see that the boat was already heading away from the island and back towards the mainland.

"I guess there's no turning back now," Julia said.

"Nope," Daniel said, pulling out his gun and checking it.

"Let's go," Wang said, glancing at them.

Together, they left the beach covering their footprints in the sand, and then entered the tree-lined area behind it. They moved slowly through the trees and the thick undergrowth heading towards the other side of the island. Almost an hour after heading inland, they had to stop as they heard men approaching from the right. They hid down behind the thick undergrowth waiting and watching, and then they saw at least six uniformed men walking in single file as if they were patrolling the island with machine guns held ready to fire. The four of them waited in silence as the uniformed patrol passed by before continuing on.

"It looks like this is really the place," Julia whispered back to Daniel who was walking behind her.

"How big an army does this organization have?" Daniel whispered back.

"I don't know," Julia whispered, continuing to follow behind both Wan and Yak. "I couldn't find out, but I know it's worldwide."

"Great!" Daniel whispered through clenched teeth.

They moved carefully through the thick undergrowth and the trees, trying not to make a noise as they went. It was about an hour later that they came across another patrol and had to stop and hide again.

Daniel moved up beside Wang, "Just how many of them are there on this island?" he whispered.

Wang glanced back at him and smiled, "I guess we're going to find out," he said.

Daniel nodded, rolling his eyes, "Right," he said.

"Are you impatient?" Julia whispered to him with a smile from behind.

Daniel glanced back at her, "Sure," he whispered. "Very impatient! Aren't you?"

Julia smiled again as Daniel turned to continue following behind both Wang and Yak.

*

Sometime later, they found themselves climbing upwards. They moved slowly, each of them now feeling tired, and then they came to a ridge. They stopped, lay down flat, then crawled forward to the edge to look down over it. Wang took out a pair of binoculars and looked through them down at the small fishing village below.

"What can you see?" Daniel asked.

"It's the fishing village," Wang said. "It's strange, it seems almost deserted as if hardly anybody lives there. There are just a few people … wait! They have guns! They're not villagers."

"So … what did they do with all of the villagers?" Julia asked.

Wang lowered the binoculars and glanced at her, "There's only one way to find out," he said. He looked at Daniel, "I'll go down, try to find out what's going on."

Daniel shook his head, he checked his watch, "It's best to wait until it's dark," he said. "You don't know what you're walking into down there."

"Look McGlade," Wang said. "That's my niece they have down there. I'm not going to wait hours for it to get dark. Who knows what they're doing to her down there?"

"Look, be sensible," Daniel said. "You have men coming later, we should wait."

"I'm going down!" Wang said. He turned to Yak, "You wait here with them."

Yak shook his head, "I go with you," he said. "Where you go, I go."

Daniel looked at Yak in surprise. It was the first time that he had heard the huge man speak.

Wang looked at his bodyguard, then smiled and placed his hand on his shoulder.

"You're a loyal friend," Wang said. "Thank you."

Yak nodded.

Wang turned to Daniel and handed him the binoculars, "You stay here with Miss Jones. Yak and I will go down."

Daniel stared at him, then took the binoculars and nodded, "Good luck," he said.

Wang smiled and nodded back, "You too," he said.

Both Daniel and Julia watched as Wang and Yak began to make their way down from the ridge towards the village below.

"He's crazy going down there in broad daylight," Julia said.

Daniel shrugged, "If it were my niece, I'd do the same," he said.

They watched them go down until they disappeared from sight. Daniel studied the village below with the binoculars then handed them to Julia.

"What do you think they do down there?" Julia said, looking through the binoculars. "The place looks so dead!"

"Your guess is as good as mine," Daniel said.

He checked his watch, "Still some time before nightfall. You might as well get some rest, I'll watch the village."

Julia handed him back the binoculars, "Thanks," she said, "but I'm not particularly tired …"

Just then, they heard shouts and then gunfire.

"Hell!" Daniel said, raising the binoculars to his eyes to look down towards the village. At first he saw nothing, then he saw some uniformed men moving into sight with both Wang and Yak between them held at gunpoint and holding their hands above their heads.

"They've got Wang and Yak," Daniel said.

Daniel heard Julia gasp as he continued watching through the binoculars.

"Are they okay?" Julia asked.

"They're okay," Daniel answered. "They've been taken prisoner. Wait! … Something's happening!"

Through the binoculars, Daniel saw Wang suddenly turn to one of the men behind him and try to wrestle the gun from him, another uniformed man ran from behind and hit Wang across the face with the butt of his machine gun. Wang fell to the ground and the uniformed man who had hit him now stood over Wang aiming his weapon down towards him preparing to fire. Yak suddenly cried out and ran forward leaping on the man as the machine gun went off. Yak's body jerked back as the bullets entered him and he fell down to the ground beside Wang, his body now covered in blood.

"Jesus!" Daniel whispered to himself, staring down at the scene through the binoculars.

"What happened?" Julia asked anxiously beside him.

Daniel watched Wang get up onto his knees and crawl forward to lean down over the body of his bodyguard and friend.

Daniel lowered the binoculars, "Yak got shot saving Wang's life," he said. "He's dead."

Julia looked at him with a worried expression.

Suddenly, they heard something behind them. They both turned as one to see four uniformed men aiming their machine guns down at them.

"Who are you?" the uniformed man in front asked.

CHAPTER 28

As they were being marched with their hands on their heads through the small fishing village, Daniel glanced both right and left looking for any sign of life but found none. The four-man patrol marched them through the village towards a large wooden building which stood in the village centre. Daniel could only imagine that it was some kind of grand village hall. They were made to enter and saw that although it was large from the outside, the inside was almost empty. The men forced them into the middle of the large hall, and then each of the men stood still with their machine guns trained on both Daniel and Julia apparently waiting for something. As he stood there with his hands on his head waiting for he didn't know what, Daniel noticed a modern camera with its red light on hanging from one of the hall's walls and aimed down towards them.

"Smile," Daniel said, turning to Julia. "We're on candid camera."

Julia looked at him, then followed his gaze up towards the camera.

"What do you think we're waiting for?" Julia said to him, staring up at the camera.

"Quiet!" the man in uniform who was standing the nearest to them barked.

Suddenly, the floor beneath them began to move. Slowly, it started to descend.

"Looks like we're on some kind of a lift," Daniel whispered to Julia.

Both of them glanced down as the floor descended slowly downwards, and then, suddenly beneath them, they saw a huge brightly-lit cavern with a smooth and shiny black floor and smooth white walls. The cavern was filled with sophisticated looking machines with various coloured lights flashing on and off and tables and desks with various computers and other kinds of machines as men busied here and there, some walking from one machine to another checking something as others sat at the desks concentrating at whatever was on the screens in front of them. Daniel noticed men in uniform with machine guns, who were obviously guards, standing around the cavern and watching the workers busy at the machines. The lift section of the floor took them all the way down to the bottom and then came to a stop. Daniel looked around as he stepped off the lift and noticed brightly-lit corridors branching off in different directions from the huge cavern. Above them, and fixed all around to the walls of the cavern was a black metal catwalk with metal stairs leading up to it. On the catwalk all around the cavern stood guards holding machine guns and looking down at the beehive of activity of the many workers in the cavern below them.

"It must be some kind of secret base," Daniel said to Julia, glancing both right and left.

"It's secret all right!" Julia said, looking around.

The uniformed men got off the lift behind them and pushed them forward, forcing them to walk across the cavern floor towards what looked like closed metal doors on the other side. Various workers here and there glanced at them as they passed, then continued on with their work. Two steel metal doors slid open as they approached them and the uniformed men behind them pushed them forward through the opening. They entered a well-lit corridor. They had only taken a few steps when another door slid open to the right and the men behind them pushed them inside. The room they entered was large and comfortably furnished with sofas, a huge desk, two bookcases filled with books, a large wall-screen and a wide window to the right which looked out onto the work-floor outside. Behind the desk sat a very fat man. In his hand his held a drink which looked like whisky in what appeared to be a pure crystal glass. Beside him, standing still as if she were standing to attention, was the tall woman named Miss Clarke whom Daniel had met before, although she was now wearing a blue silk Chinese costume. Nearby her, sitting in an armchair, was the thin man named Baines whom Daniel had also met before. He sat with an unpleasant looking smile on his face as he stared up at both Daniel and Julia who were being pushed forward towards the desk. The fat man sipped his drink as they entered then smiled at them amiably.

"Ah! More guests!" he said.

He shooed away the uniformed men with his hand and the men left the room. Daniel looked behind him and saw a huge blonde man standing inside the room beside the door. His large muscled arms were folded as he stared sternly and in silence at both Daniel and Julia.

"Please, sit down," the fat man said, gesturing towards two empty armchairs in front of his desk. Both Daniel and Julia moved forward and sat down in the armchairs.

"Nice to see you again," Miss Clarke said, staring coldly at Julia.

Julia returned her stare, "I'm afraid I can't say the same," she said.

A smile appeared on Miss Clarke's face breaking her cold look of ice.

"I'm sure Felicity will be pleased to see you too," she said calmly.

Julia glanced down and seemed to shudder involuntarily.

"Mr. McGlade," the fat man said, eyeing Daniel with an amiable smile. "You've led us on a merry-go-round, but we finally got what we wanted."

"What do you want with the girl?" Daniel asked.

"Ah, I see you're a man who likes to be direct Mr. McGlade. I like that, so few people are direct these days."

He leaned forward, placing his hands onto the desk.

"Let it not be said that I am an unfair man. As you are going to die, I see no reason why I should not, let's say, divulge a few secrets, eh?"

Both Daniel and Julia stared at him in silence waiting for him to continue.

"Look outside the window Mr. McGlade. Tell me what you see."

Daniel looked towards the window, then stood up and walked over to it.

Julia stood up and was about to join him.

"Not you!" said the fat man, whose amiable smile suddenly disappeared as he regarded her. Julia sat back down and glanced towards Daniel.

"I see a lot of idiots running around doing nothing much," Daniel said. "If I were further away they'd look just like ants, only maybe slightly less intelligent."

The fat man chuckled.

"Yes, I heard you had a sense of humour McGlade, black though it may be. But then, you are known to be The Black Cat, are you not?"

Daniel turned and glanced back down at him.

"That's what people called me when I was boxing," he said.

"And a name well deserved, I am sure. You see Hugo over there?" the fat man said, gesturing towards the huge and silent blonde man standing by the door.

Daniel turned to look at the huge man called Hugo.

"He's a fighter too," the fat man said. "I'm sure he'd just love to have a chance at fighting you."

"Sorry," Daniel said. "I gave up boxing."

"Is that … fear perhaps?" the fat man asked, eyeing Daniel carefully.

Daniel shook his head, "No, I just wouldn't want to embarrass him in front of his friends."

The huge man called Hugo snarled and made a move towards Daniel.

"Hugo! Stop!" the fat man said, raising a hand towards him. "You can have fun with our guest later."

Hugo stopped but remained staring bitterly across at Daniel.

"You must be careful what you say to, or about, Hugo," the fat man said to Daniel. "He can be a trifle sensitive, and very dangerous."

"Sounds like you should put him on a leash," Daniel said, staring back at Hugo. He turned and looked back through the window at the people working at the various machines and computers in the huge cavern outside.

"Business is my business Mr. McGlade," the fat man said, observing Daniel as he stood by the window. "Business is our business, this organization's business. Do you think it is governments, politicians, who rule the world? There are people working for us who would surprise you Mr. McGlade. People will do anything for money, money and power."

Daniel turned once again to look back at him, "I'm not surprised you're fat!" he said. "You're full of hot air!"

The fat man dropped his smile and stared back into Daniel's eyes.

"What do you want with the girl?" Daniel asked for the second time.

There was a silence as the fat man continued to stare up at him, then a smile came back onto his face.

"Nuclear weapons control the world. We are currently tracking down and finding the location of every nuclear missile in the world."

Daniel stared at him for a moment.

"What do you intend to do?" he asked finally. "Blow us all up?"

The fat man chuckled once more.

"Au contraire, Mr. McGlade. We intend to control them. You see, a device has been invented to render useless any nuclear weapon, completely and utterly useless."

He remained staring up at Daniel, observing his reaction before continuing.

"Do you know what that means?" he asked.

Daniel stared back at him thoughtfully.

"Powerful countries and anybody else would be made vulnerable," he said.

"Very, very vulnerable," the fat man said, eyeing Daniel carefully. "Have you any idea how much the countries concerned would pay to stop such an event from happening?"

Daniel nodded, "A lot of peanuts," he said.

The fat man chuckled again, "That's right Mr. McGlade, an awful lot of peanuts."

"So, what does this have to do with the girl?"

The fat man stared at him, his smile now disappearing again.

"We discovered that she has, or knows, the whereabouts of this invention."

Daniel glanced away and let out a long sigh, "Got it," he said.

"Have you?" the fat man asked. "Have you really got it?"

Daniel looked back at him.

"What do you mean?" he asked.

The fat man shrugged, "Oh, but of course. You can't remember anything! How unfortunate. Apparently, the invention has been hidden, something to do with a 'butterfly' I believe. Do you know anything about that Mr. McGlade?"

Daniel grinned, then chuckled himself.

"Can't get her to talk, eh?"

"She proves to be … very stubborn, just like her father."

"Her father?" Daniel said. "Did you kill him too?"

"Oh no Mr. McGlade, her father is very much alive, although, a little damaged for wear. You see, he's been tortured. Yes, unfortunately a most stubborn man. At the moment, he's enjoying some time in one of our … er, dungeons."

"I'm sure he is!" Daniel said bitterly, staring back down at the fat man.

"We did manage to find out however that somehow he managed to hide the invention with the girl before sending her out of the country … to you."

Daniel's mouth open in surprise as he continued to stare down at the fat man.

"Why?" he asked. "Why would he send her to me?"

"Precisely my question," the fat man said. He leaned forward pointing a stubby finger towards Daniel. "Why would he send his daughter to a

Mr. Daniel McGlade? I was … naturally curious, so I did some digging into your past. We discovered that you grew up in an orphanage that you ran away from. Later, you learned to fight and became a boxer, a notable one whom they called 'The Black Cat'. Then later you joined the police, and now, you're a private eye. So … what possible connection could Suzie's father have with you? Then it came to me. I discovered the secret visits that Suzie's mother made to your orphanage, visits, I believe, you knew nothing about."

He paused, staring directly into Daniel's eyes.

"Do you see … where I'm going Mr. McGlade?"

Daniel stared back at him in silence.

His mouth opened as if he were going to say something, but nothing came out. He suddenly gazed around the room, looking at everything and nothing as a sudden realization came to him like a lightning bolt from the dark.

"He … he's my father," Daniel said to himself, almost in a whisper.

The fat man nodded, staring at him intensely.

"It would appear so," he said.

"That means …" Daniel began.

"That Suzie is … your sister," the fat man said, finishing Daniel's sentence for him. "Or more precisely … half-sister."

Daniel suddenly looked shattered, as if he were about to fall.

The fat man turned, glancing across at Hugo, "Take our Mr. McGlade down to his father's cell, would you Hugo?"

Hugo nodded and spoke into a small communicator.

"As for you my dear …" the fat man said, turning to Julia who'd been sitting and listening to the whole conversation with interest, "I believe Felicity would be most pleased to keep you entertained."

Julia's eyes widened in fear.

"No! … Please!" Julia cried out.

The fat man smiled, then waved his hand towards her in dismissal, "Take her away!" he said.

CHAPTER 29

Daniel was pushed into the darkened cell. He turned just as the metal door slammed shut behind him. He stood for a moment, looking at the closed cell door, then he heard a sound in one corner of the cell and quickly glanced round towards it. He peered in the semi-darkness, trying to adjust his eyes to the lack of light. In a far corner of the cell, he saw a bearded man in chains. He was thin and barely clothed. Daniel hesitated, then slowly stepped towards him. He stared down at the man's face as he approached him. The face looked tired and worn, timid and lifeless. His thin body seemed frail as if life had been sucked out of him. Daniel crouched down in front of him, staring at the pitiful form of the man who sat chained to the wall and staring blankly in front of him on the hard stone floor. Tears came into Daniel's eyes as he stared at the man's face. Slowly, he reached out a hand and gently touched the man's cheek.

"D … dad?" he said, half choking on the words as he spoke.

"D … dad? Is … is it … really you?"

The man's eyes looked slowly up and into his. Recognition showed behind them, and then suddenly, the man's face broke into a smile.

"S ... son?" he said weakly. "Daniel? ... My ... my son?"

Then he slowly raised his arms up towards Daniel as if he were trying to reach forward and hug him.

"Dad! ... Father!" Daniel cried out, falling forward into his father's arms and hugging him as tightly as he could. Years of pain and torment suddenly burst from him in an explosion of tears and sobs that now completely racked his body.

"Dad! ... Dad! ..." he cried.

*

The fat man leaned back in his chair watching the screen up on the wall in front of him.

"How very touching," he said coldly.

He turned to the thin man named Baines who was sitting and looking up at the screen nearby, "Go see how the men are progressing with the girl Suzie," he said.

Baines nodded, standing up from his chair.

"We must find the whereabouts of the invention as quickly as possible," the fat man said thoughtfully.

*

When Daniel finally stopped sobbing, he pulled himself back and wiped the tears from his face.

"They ... they hurt you?" he asked, gazing at the marks on his father's body.

His father managed to shake his head, "Doesn't matter. I must ... I must tell you ... why ... why I left you behind."

Tears still fell down onto Daniel's cheeks as he gazed into his father's eyes.

"I was ... a member of Spider," his father said. "Your mother ... she was a member too. We ... we were married secretly."

He paused, gazing down.

"Something ... something happened. I ... I couldn't do the things they asked me to do any longer. I ... I decided to leave, but ... but my wife, your mother, she refused. I ... I tried to make her ... make her leave ... then they found out and ... I ... I staged our deaths ... yours and ... and mine ... but ... I ... couldn't take you with me. I had to ... to leave you behind ... had to ... hide you. I left you ... in an orphanage ... then I ... I escaped. I met Lin and .... together we had a daughter, staying hidden in Hong Kong. Sometimes, Lin ... would visit the orphanage for me ... to see if you were okay. Sorry ... but ... I never forgot you! Never forgot you son! You ... you've grown into such a ... a fine boy!"

"Oh dad!" Daniel said, then quickly grabbed his father and hugged him tightly once more.

"It ... it's okay! It's okay dad! It ... it's okay."

Daniel began to sob once more, holding his father tightly in his arms.

Suddenly, the cell door opened and a shaft of light cut through the darkness entering the cell from the corridor outside.

"It's time to go!" said Hugo's harsh voice.

Daniel glanced back up at him, his eyes and face filled with tears as he continued to sob and hug his father tightly.

CHAPTER 30

The large room looked something like an arena. People were sitting around on benches that had been placed in a circle to create a wide open space in the middle. There were people in business suits, people in white coats looking like scientists, and people in uniform. Around the outside of the circle, behind the benches, there were other uniformed men, guards, with their weapons ready.

Hugo pushed Daniel through a gap in the benches and into the centre of the 'arena'.

Daniel looked round at the surrounding people, then turned to face Hugo.

"What's going to happen here?" he asked.

Hugo smiled, "We're going to have some fun,' he said. "But first …"

Hugo clicked his fingers. There was a commotion as guards came into the room pushing four men in front of them. Daniel stared at the men, a surprised look on his face, as the men were pushed with their hands tied behind their backs into the arena.

"Heller!" Daniel gasped in surprise.

Heller stopped in front of him and stood looking at him, "Hello McGlade. Nice to see you again."

Hugo pushed him in the back.

"No talking!" he shouted. "Mr. X is going to say something!"

A huge screen on the far wall suddenly came to life. Daniel stared up at the screen and saw the features of the fat man gazing down at them.

"My friends," the fat man started. "Today is a special day. We have traitors to deal with, people who are thorns in our side. Some of you may know Miss Jones …"

The screen's image changed and now showed a picture of Julia tied with her arms above her. She was hanging from a hook which hung down from the ceiling with her feet barely touching the floor. The fear in her face was plain to see as she struggled in vain to free herself.

"Julia!" Daniel breathed, taking one step closer towards the screen as he stared up at it.

"Miss Jones is a traitor," the fat man continued. "Believe me, her fate will be one worse than death. Death? She will pray for it to come!"

The image changed back to show his face once more.

"And there are those who are thorns in our side. Take the four men who have been pushed into the arena for example."

All eyes went to Heller and his three men, Stone, Knife and the man in the smart suit. Only Heller's fourth man, the tall man, was missing.

"They have their own little organization going, although, not quite so big as ours of course. It appears they'd heard that the young girl, Suzie, was worth quite a lot to us. They sought to find her themselves, tried to find out why she was so valuable, possibly use her for trade … they were dealing in our affairs, and that cannot be tolerated! So, we have decided to make an example of them. Here is a message … to anyone, anyone who wishes to deal in our affairs again."

Daniel jerked his head round as he heard the click of a gun being made ready to fire. He was just in time to see Hugo fire the first shot into Stone's head. As Stone's lifeless body crumpled to the floor amidst the screams of Heller and his other men, Hugo aimed again and this time fired into the man in the smart suit's face. Blood splattered out onto Knife's face and clothes as he stood nearby, his mouth gaping open in an expression of shock. He watched with horror as the second man's body fell down to the floor beside him and then with terror-filled eyes he raised his hands which were shaking with fear.

"No! No! Please! Don't shoot! Please!" he said, his voice trembling as he spoke, staring at Hugo who was now aiming the gun towards him.

The shot rang out as Hugo fired and the bullet entered Knife's forehead, jerking his head grotesquely back causing blood to spurt out before he fell to the floor dead. Heller remained still, staring down at his three men with a look of shock on his blood splattered face.

Hugo smiled, studying his shocked expression, then raised the gun and aimed it towards him.

"Now, now Hugo," the fat man's voice said, staring down at the scene from the screen on the wall.

"Not Mr. Heller. He may prove to be valuable to us."

Hugo continued to stare at Heller, then slowly lowered the gun.

"Mr. Heller," the fat man's voice said.

Heller stared down at the dead bodies of his men, then looked up at the fat man on the screen.

"It appears you have connections that we would be most interested in using. If you agree to work with us, rather than against us, we will spare your life."

"You killed my men!" Heller said bitterly up to the screen.

"And we will kill you too, have no doubt about it. So, what is it to be Mr. Heller? Work with us, or die now?"

Heller glanced back down at the lifeless bodies of his men lying at his feet.

"Do I have a choice?" he said.

"No, I'm afraid you don't," the fat man said. "Just bear in mind how we treat traitors, or anyone who goes against us, and we may get along just fine. And now, Hugo, you may continue with your … fun!"

Hugo grinned and motioned for guards to drag the three bodies out of the arena. He turned and gestured for two other guards to escort Heller away with them.

There was whispering and soft murmuring of the surrounding crowd airing fears as they sat on the benches watching the bodies of the men being dragged away in front of them.

Hugo turned to face Daniel with a grin, "Now, let's see how good you really are," he said, staring across the arena and into Daniel's eyes.

Daniel stared back at him, then raised his fists prepared to fight.

CHAPTER 31

The crowd cheered as Hugo punched Daniel in the face two successive times knocking Daniel back. Daniel remained on his feet, ducked to avoid another punch and then threw one of his own which caught Hugo on the jaw. Hugo touched his jaw grinning, then quickly closed in grabbing Daniel in his two hugely muscled arms. Daniel cried out as Hugo began to squeeze him. For a moment, he hung limply, his feet not touching the floor, feeling his life being squeezed out of him as if he were in the grip of some giant-sized python. Daniel let out a yell, then suddenly swung his head forward and caught Hugo on the nose. Hugo cried out and lost his grip, dropping Daniel and staggering back as blood now spurted out of his nose.

*

Felicity stared up at the screen on the wall watching the fight with interest. The room in which she stood was smaller. She turned to face Julia, who was tied helplessly in front of her hanging from a hook. Julia pulled without success at the ropes binding her wrists above her.

"Your boyfriend's faring quite well against our blonde giant," Felicity said.

Julia shot her a glance.

"He's not my boyfriend!" she said.

Felicity smiled stepping closer to her.

"No? Well, then … maybe you wish he were?" she asked, an amusing tone to her voice.

She moved closer and placed her mouth beside Julia's ear.

"And … what are we going to do with you?" she said softly. "I have some new toys I haven't tried out yet. Some things I'd like to … play with."

Julia turned her head away from the screen showing the fight and spat in her face. Felicity quickly pulled her head back and closed her eyes, then she wiped her face with the back of her hand.

"You will regret that!" she said menacingly, staring coldly into Julia's eyes.

Felicity turned and walked over to a large box on a nearby table. She gazed down into the box.

"Let's see now … what shall I use?"

She placed a finger to her lips as if she were finding it difficult to decide what to choose.

"Ah! Yes!" she reached into the box and took out a large knife, then she turned to face Julia with the knife in her hand. Felicity smiled, studying

Julia's expression of fear as she stared at knife's long blade in Felicity's hand which gleamed in the overhead lights.

"Yes, I think this will be perfect," Felicity said, now making her way back across the room to Julia. She stopped in front of Julia's helplessly bound body and placed the blade of the knife in front of Julia's face. Felicity saw the fear in Julia's eyes as she played with the knife, first holding it first in front of Julia's right cheek, and then her left. Julia pushed her head back away from the knife's blade as far as she could, her eyes widened in fear as she stared helplessly at the blade in front of her. Felicity grinned, then lowered the knife down away from her face and began cutting at Julia's red-check shirt. She cut the fabric of the shirt all the way down past each button until the shirt was completely open, next, she opened the shirt up wider to gaze at Julia's body.

Felicity studied her for a moment, then placed a hand against her. Julia gasped, trying to jerk away from Felicity's touch. Felicity grinned, letting her hand roam lazily around Julia's body.

"So much fear!" Felicity said, moving closer to her and purring as if she were a cat.

Julia gasped again and Felicity smiled, observing Julia's reaction to her touch.

"Do you know what I like?" Felicity whispered, leaning close to Julia's ear to her with a smile on her face. "No?" Felicity giggled. "Well .. you're going to find out. You see, they told me I could kill you, but I like to play first."

Julia gasped again.

Felicity leaned back and grinned at her, "And I have such a good imagination!" she said.

She glanced down, then took the knife and cut through Julia's belt.

Felicity gazed back up at her, looking with a grin into Julia's eyes, "What will we find underneath?" she asked playfully.

She lowered her head again and began cutting through the fabric of Julia's jeans.

"Please!" Julia said. shaking her head.

"Oh, don't spoil my fun!" Felicity said, grinning back up at her. "I've barely started with you! They tell me that you're some kind of a spy, a naughty spy! I expected spies to be stronger than that! Oh, look! You're beginning to cry! Oh, isn't that sweet!"

Felicity finished cutting through Julia's jeans and pulled them roughly off her body. Felicity stood back to study her, toying with the knife in her hand as tears now streamed down Julia's face.

"Please!" Julia said again, her voice now breaking and her body visibly trembling as she spoke.

Felicity studied her for a moment more, then turned away from her and strode back to the table nearby. She placed the knife down onto the table, then took something from out of the box. As she turned back once again to face Julia, Julia saw the whip that Felicity was now holding in her hands.

Felicity smiled across at her as Julia stared with tear-stained and fear-filled eyes at the whip.

Felicity's smile widened, "Naughty spy!" she said softly, then she giggled again.

As Felicity slowly walked back towards her, Julia began to shake her head and whimper as she pulled helplessly at her bonds.

*

Daniel fell to the floor gasping. His face was now a bloody mess. Hugo stood over him, sneering down at him. Blood trickled down from the corner of his mouth and his nose. A bruise had appeared on the side of his face beside a cut.

"Is that all you've got? Huh?" Hugo said, kicking Daniel in the ribs. "Where's this famous Black Cat I've heard so much about? The guy who always bounces back up? Eh?"

He kicked Daniel again.

Daniel grunted, then tried to push himself up from the floor.

Hugo laughed. He turned and called to one of the guards.

"Bring the prisoner!" he ordered.

Daniel was still trying to push himself up onto his feet when two guards returned holding onto a prisoner between them. The prisoner could barely stand up on his feet as the two guards kept their hold on him, keeping him from falling. Daniel glanced up through his one good eye which had not been beaten to closing and saw his father.

"Shall we make this more interesting McGlade?" Hugo said down to him. "I think you need something to give you an extra burst of adrenaline!"

He turned as one of the guards handed him a gun.

"Let's see if we can find something to stimulate you, shall we?" Hugo said with a grin.

Daniel watched as Hugo walked over to his father and put the gun to his father's head.

Hugo turned and looked down at Daniel with his grin.

"Say goodbye to daddy!" he said.

Daniel screamed out.

"Nooooo!!"

Hugo fired the gun

Blood spurted out of the other side of his father's head as Daniel screamed out at the word 'father' at the top of his lungs. He froze, watching his father's body fall to the floor as if in slow motion, a lifeless body falling down into a puddle of its own blood.

"Noooooo!!"

Daniel continued to scream.

Suddenly, he found himself up on his feet and running towards Hugo who had now thrown the gun aside. Daniel leapt into him, punching with all his might as the huge blonde man fell to the floor. Daniel cried out, punching and punching as if he had suddenly become insane. His punches hit Hugo's body and Hugo's face as Hugo now began to cry out beneath him trying to defend himself from the rain of blows which fell relentlessly down on him again and again without letting up. When Hugo's face was a bloody mess and a blow to his chest made it difficult for him to breathe, guards ran forward and tried to pull a crazed and insane Daniel McGlade up off him as Daniel continued to beat down at the blonde giant even after Hugo had lost consciousness.

*

"Oh my God," the fat man breathed, staring up at the screen on the wall of his office with a look of shock on his face from behind his desk.

Baines, the thin man, suddenly burst into the room.

"We've found it!" he blurted out. "The Butterfly! We've found it!"

The fat man's mouth seemed to drop open, then, with surprising speed for a man of his weight, he stood up and moved around the desk heading for the door.

*

The guards pulled Daniel out of the arena and away from Hugo's now badly beaten and unconscious body.

"Take him away!" the head guard shouted, as he gazed back down at Hugo's body in disbelief. The guard stood shaking his head. To him and to everybody else who had met Hugo, the huge man-monster had always seemed invincible.

CHAPTER 32

Julia, hung from the hook sobbing and screaming hysterically as Felicity stood in front of her, now jabbing a red electrified trident at her body.

Felicity giggled as Julia begged and whimpered for her to stop.

After a moment, Felicity stopped jabbing her and leaned towards her, "You've already told me everything I wanted to know little Miss secret agent! Now … I don't need to know anything! Nothing at all! I'm just enjoying myself! You can understand that, can't you?"

She touched Julia with the trident again, and once again giggled as Julia screamed out loudly, jerking helplessly in her bonds.

Suddenly, a man in a uniform entered the room. He froze in his tracks, hesitating as he stared across at Julia being tortured. Felicity stopped what she was doing and turned to face him.

"Well? What is it?" she asked, observing the man's open-mouthed expression. "I thought I gave instructions not to be disturbed when I'm amusing myself!"

The uniformed man glanced down as if he were embarrassed, "I … I'm sorry," he said. "But … but the other prisoner's ready."

A smile came to Felicity's lips, "The other prisoner?" she said. "You mean … McGlade?"

The uniformed man nodded, "He … he is ready," he said.

Felicity smiled, "Good", she said thoughtfully. She nodded to the man, "You may go!" she said.

She watched as the man quickly turned and left, then looked back at Julia, "I'm afraid I have to go," she said. "But don't worry, I'll be back! I have other games to play with your boyfriend!"

She remained still, studying the way Julia now hung sobbing and crying uncontrollably, then stepped towards her slowly.

"You're such a weak creature," she said. "You were so easy to break. You're so pathetic! I'm surprised they allowed you to be a secret agent. You told me everything I wanted to know in the first ten minutes!" Felicity giggled, "Maybe your boyfriend will be more fun! When I come back, I'll punish you some more, in fact … I tell a lie. I'm going to punish you a 'lot' more, for being so weak! Believe me, I have a lot more toys to try out on you!"

Felicity giggled again as she remained staring at Julia.

"See you soon!" she said, then turned and left the room.

*

The fat man walked quickly towards the end of the corridor and entered the room which resembled a large lab with white walls and a white polished floor. He strode over to the two men who were standing nearby a stainless steel metal-top table. Bound to the table face down with her wrists and ankles tied firmly to the four corners was Suzie, the young Chinese girl.

"Has she talked? Has she?" the fat man asked excitedly. "The Butterfly! What is it? Where are the plans for the invention?"

"You moved so fast, you didn't give me time to explain," Baines said, following behind him into the lab and now walking up beside him.

The fat man turned to him.

"The Butterfly! What is it? Tell me! I must know!"

Baines smiled, "The kid's stubborn, very stubborn, but finally we broke her."

"Well? Where is it?" the fat man shouted, staring at him impatiently. "The Butterfly!"

Baines grinned, "it's somewhere we would never have thought of looking!' he said.

"I'm warning you Baines!' the fat man shouted, staring at him angrily. "Just tell me where it is!"

Baines nodded at one of the men behind him and the man nodded back and stepped towards the table. The man grinned as he reached forward and slowly lifted Suzie's plaid skirt back up towards her waist.

Suzie began to whimper and her body began to shake as the fat man moved forward, his mouth slightly open in both shock and surprise as he stared down at the butterfly tattoo he could now see tattooed onto Suzie's upper left thigh. The butterfly looked beautiful, colourful, and had been expertly tattooed onto her.

"The Butterfly!" the fat man gasped, now reaching his hand out towards it.

Suzie cried out, pulling strongly at the ropes binding her wrists and ankles in place as she felt the fat man's fingers now gently caressing the colourful butterfly

"There is a micro-chip beneath it," Baines said from behind him. "It was cleverly hidden, no one would have thought to look for it ..."

"Get it out," the fat man said softly, before Baines could finish his sentence.

"Well, we can," Baines said, "but ..."

The fat man now turned to him and

shouted, "Get it out! Get it out now!"

"But ... we need a doctor," Baines said. "She needs an operation, without it, it will scar ..."

The fat man advanced towards him.

"Do I look like a man who cares about some sniveling schoolgirl? I said, get it out, now! Use a knife! Carve it out of her! I don't care how you do it! But get it out!"

Baines glanced nervously at the other two men. Suddenly, the fat man smiled as a thought came to him.

"No … wait. Get Heller. Get him in here! Now!"

His smile turned into a grin as he gazed back down at the beautifully tattooed butterfly on Suzie's left thigh.

"We can kill two birds with one stone," he said.

CHAPTER 33

Daniel hung from the ceiling with his wrists tied above him and his feet barely touching the floor. Bruises and blood covered his face as he hung with his head lowered. The small room was bare, except for one wooden table and two wooden chairs. Suddenly, the door to the room opened. Felicity stepped inside and stood for a moment looking at Daniel, then slowly she walked towards him. Behind her was a guard carrying her box of 'toys'. He headed towards the table and placed the box onto the table-top, then he turned and left the room, glancing back at both Felicity and Daniel as he went.

Felicity stood in front of Daniel. She studied his battered face and his blood-soaked clothes before speaking.

"I saw what you did to Hugo," she said. "That was impressive."

Daniel raised his head to look at her.

Felicity moved closer to him.

"But here …" she said, in a soft voice, "… here, you are my prisoner. And with my toys …" she gestured towards the box on the table, "… I can do with you whatever I want."

She moved closer towards him, "Really … whatever I want!" she giggled. "And you …. you can't do a thing to stop me, not even when …" she touched his face gently, "… you're screaming and begging for me to stop."

Felicirty giggled again.

Daniel kept silent, continuing to look at her.

"You know, your girlfriend told me everything," Felicity said in a soft voice. "I made her cry. She's crying in the other room right now like a little schoolgirl. I made her beg McGlade! Beg like a little girl! I do hope you're stronger than her. I don't want you to beg too soon, you see, it would spoil my pleasure!"

Slowly, she reached her hands towards him, grabbed his shirt, and then ripped it open, the buttons flying quickly off it and onto the floor.

"She begged me to stop, but …" Felicity giggled, "I didn't, of course! I continued. You see, I enjoy that!"

"You really are one sick bitch!" Daniel said, staring into her eyes with his one good eye that hadn't closed from swelling.

Felicity held his shirt open and studied his chest. She ran her right hand down over it softly.

"Yes," she said with a grin. "Many people have told me that. They said I was sick, but later, they regretted it. Oh, you couldn't imagine how they regretted it! How I made them regret it!" She giggled again. "And now … I'm going to have fun with you, McGlade. Torturing men, it's so much more … interesting!"

Daniel tried to move, tried to free himself from the ropes binding his wrists above his head, but it was no use.

Felicity laughed, "Go ahead, try to free yourself! You want to! But I'm afraid you've been tied too tightly. You see? There's no escape for you McGlade, no escape! You're completely helpless, completely in my power … and I'm going to enjoy every second … every …" she leaned forward and planted a kiss on his chest, "… single second!"

Daniel struggled futilely in his bonds as she continued to kiss and caress his chest.

"How does it feel to be helpless?" she asked, now gazing into his eyes with a devilish grin. "I know how to break a man … make him beg … and even … make him cry!"

Daniel stared at her.

"You don't believe me?" her grin widened.

She glanced downwards.

"Let's see …"

Slowly, she reached down and undid Daniel's belt. She looked up at him and poked her tongue through her teeth as she continued grinning like a little girl about to open a present.

"You really are sick!" Daniel said, continuing to stare at her.

Felicity stared at him, "That's the second time you said that," she said, now sounding slightly annoyed. "I am seriously going to enjoy breaking you!"

Slowly, she reached down with her hand as she continued gazing into his eyes. Daniel gasped and tried to move his body back away from her.

"Where are you going?" she said softly, the grin once again on her face. "You're not going anywhere. I have you … exactly where I want you!"

Daniel squeezed his eyes shut.

"I hope you remember this," Felicity whispered to him softly, "just before I kill you!"

Daniel gasped again and he now heard Felicity laughing.

Suddenly, he opened his eyes and spat into her face.

Felicity stopped what she was doing to him and stared at him angrily.

"You're going to pay for that!" she said bitterly, wiping her face. "I am definitely going to enjoy making you beg!"

She turned quickly and walked over to the table and her box of 'toys'.

Suddenly, the door of the room opened and Miss Clarke stepped in. Felicity turned to look at her.

"Leave him!" Miss Clarke ordered, walking over to her.

Felicity gazed at her with a shocked expression on her face.

"What …? Wh … why? I thought you told me I could play with him!"

"Go!" Miss Clarke said sternly, pointing towards the door.

"But …!"

"I said go!"

Felicity gazed back at her for a moment, then took one last look at Daniel before reluctantly turning and striding across the room towards the door.

Miss Clarke watched her go, and when the door had shut behind her, she turned to look at Daniel.

"Who are you?" she asked, walking slowly over towards him.

Daniel stared at her.

"What?" he said, surprised at the question.

"Who are you? Daniel McGlade is not your real name, is it?"

Daniel continued to stare at her for a moment, then shrugged as best as he could.

"What do you care? Why don't you just kill me and have done with it?"

Miss Clarke stopped walking forward and now stood in front of him. She reached out a hand and lifted his chin to study his face.

"What ... what relation were you to the prisoner? The ... the man Hugo killed?"

Daniel studied her face, there was something earnest in the way she was asking.

"You don't know?" he asked. "The fat man knows. You were there, you heard what he said."

"Is ... is it true?" Miss Clark asked.

"Why don't you ask him?" Daniel said.

Miss Clarke glanced down, "He ... he doesn't tell me everything. Just ... just before the prisoner was killed ... you ... you shouted out something. You ... you said ..."

"Father," Daniel said, finishing her sentence for her.

Miss Clarke's eyes suddenly jumped up to gaze into his.

"But ... but that's impossible! My son ... my son died! He died!"

Suddenly, Daniel stared at her in shock. He saw tears forming in Miss Clarke's eyes, and then the realization struck him, the realization of just who was there, right at that moment, standing in front of him.

"Y ... you're ... my mother?" he said, incredulously.

Miss Clark shook her head, "No! No! It's not possible! My son died! He ...!"

"Oh my God!" Daniel breathed softly to himself as he stared at her. "I ... I was put in an orphanage to be hidden from you ... from the organization! It was the only way ... the only way he could escape and ... and save himself, and me!"

Miss Clarke looked up into Daniel's eyes. Tears were now running down her cheeks.

"He ... he wanted to leave the organization. I ... I wouldn't go ... I knew the danger ..."

"Mother?" Daniel said softly, almost to himself. "Did ... did you know the that the prisoner was ... was your husband?"

Miss Clarke stared at him as tears ran down her cheeks, then she shook her head, "I only just found out," she said, "when they brought him out. They ... they hid his identity from me. And then ... when I saw him ...!"

She glanced down as a sob racked her body. She stood for a moment crying as Daniel watched her with a look of shock on his face, then she looked back up at him and moved closer to touch his face gently. She stood gazing at his features, then reached into her pocket and took out a knife. Daniel watched as she leaned up and cut the rope tying his wrists. Daniel almost fell as he came down onto his feet and Miss Clarke moved forward to catch him. For a moment, time seemed to freeze as they stood there, gazing into each other's eyes.

"You … you look just like your sister," Miss Clarke said.

"Suzie?" Daniel said. "But … she's half Chinese."

Miss Clarke shook her head, "No … your twin sister."

Daniel stared at her open-mouthed, "My …?"

"We had twins. Your father took you, the boy, but the girl stayed with me."

"I … I have a twin sister?" Daniel said loudly, staring wide-eyed into his mother's eyes.

Miss Clarke nodded with a slight smile on her lips.

"You were just with her," she said.

Daniel stared back at her letting the words sink in.

"F … Felicity? Felicity is my … twin sister?" he asked in total shock and disbelief.

Miss Clark nodded, "I should have seen the resemblance earlier … but, your face was so bruised…"

Daniel gazed down thoughtfully.

"Now, I … I understand," he said. "There … there was … something about her …"

Daniel," his mother said, grasping his arms tightly. "You have to leave. They're going to kill you, you and your friends."

She took a gun from out of her pocket.

"Here, take this! They have most of the fishing village prisoners in some cells further along the corridor to the left."

She handed him a set of keys.

"You can free them. They'll want their revenge, some of them were killed. You can escape in the commotion."

Daniel glanced down at the keys before taking them.

"But … you!" he said. "I … I can't leave you here! Not now! I … I've just found you!"

Tears once more fell onto Miss Clarke's cheeks as she gazed into his eyes.

"My son!" she said, almost choking on the words as she leaned forward to hug him tightly.

Gently, she kissed his cheek, then leaned back and gazed once more into his eyes.

"Go!" she said. "Go now! I will be okay."

Reluctantly, Daniel broke away from her. He gazed at her for a moment, then turned and went towards the door. As he reached it, he glanced back at her. His mother remained standing there, completely still, her hands clasped together as tears streamed down her face. Daniel paused, taking the image of his mother standing there and tearfully gazing at him in his mind, and then he turned and left the room.

CHAPTER 34

Heller came into the lab gazing around and saw the fat man standing next to Baines. As he walked further into the lab followed by the guard who had gone to get him, he noticed the metal table and the young Chinese girl wearing a school uniform who was lying face down, bound to it with her wrists and ankles tied to each of the table's four corners. He stared at her, and especially at the tattoo of a butterfly on her upper left thigh. He knew that the girl was Suzie Q, even though he had never met her, it was logical. Suzie lay sobbing and whimpering, hiding her face with shame away from the surrounding men.

"Beating up little girls now, huh?" Heller said, looking at the fat man.

The fat man smiled, "I daresay you've done worse. I have a job for you. Apart from your … er … clandestine activities, I understand you are quite something of a butcher."

Heller stared at him, "Dealing in meat is my trade," he said.

"Good," the fat man said. "Then you won't mind carving something out of this delectable creature's left thigh!"

Heller remained staring at him, then turned and glanced once again down at the whimpering and sobbing little Suzie tied down helplessly to the metal table-top.

He looked back up at the fat man.

"You're joking!" he said.

The fat man suddenly became deadly serious.

"On the contrary Mr. Heller. I never joke. There is a micro-chip hidden, imbedded, just beneath that exquisite butterfly tattoo. Normally, a surgeon would remove it leaving no trace of a scar, but we have neither a surgeon, nor any medical equipment to deal with such an operation on the island, and quite frankly, even if we had, I wouldn't waste time waiting for ether the surgeon or such equipment. I need that chip out of her, and I need it now!"

He moved forward and handed Heller a large knife.

"You want to work for the organization? Benefit from its enormous projects? Become … very rich? Then prove yourself! If you have to cut that little girl's thigh up into little pieces, I don't care! But get that chip out of her!"

Heller paused, staring into the fat man's eyes before taking the knife.

"Why don't you do it?" he asked. "If you want it so badly?"

The fat man moved closer, his face going red in an anger bordering on fury.

"I pay people to do things like this Mr. Heller!" he said bitterly.

He held out the knife closer towards him.

"Now do it!" he shouted. "If you don't, you will die, and someone else will do it anyway!"

Heller stared at him coldly for a moment, then he reached out and took the knife.

"Good!" The fat man said, then he turned to leave the room.

"Bring it to me as soon as you retrieve it!" he called back as he reached the door.

Heller watched him go, then looked back down at Suzie attached helplessly to the table. Suzie lay sobbing, her body shaking uncontrollably with fear as Heller now gripped the knife tightly in his hand and moved towards her.

*

Daniel advanced along the corridor.

He reached a nearby door and leaned against it, listening. From inside, he thought he could hear someone crying. He turned the door's handle and was surprised to find that the door was unlocked. Slowly, he pushed the door open and saw Julia. She was hanging limply with her hands tied above her to a hook. Her body shook as she cried and sobbed, her eyes closed tightly shut with tears running down her cheeks. Felicity was right, Daniel thought, as he entered the room and ran over to her, limping slightly on his left foot, she was crying just as if she were a little girl.

He wondered just what Felicity had done to her. As he reached her, he began undoing the ropes which bound her wrists and ankles to the bars.

"No! Don't! No more! Please! No!! No!! I beg you!! No more!! Please!! Please!!" Julia began to scream as Daniel busied himself untying the knots.

"Julia! It's me!" Daniel said.

But Julia either didn't hear him or was in too much of a shocked state to understand.

"Julia! Julia!" Daniel said as Julia began to shriek and scream.

"Julia! It's Daniel! Open your eyes Julia! Look at me! Look at me!"

Slowly, Julia calmed down, and then she opened her eyes. She saw Daniel in front of her.

"D … D … Daniel?" she managed to say, her voice still choked from sobbing as she spoke.

Daniel glanced up at her, "Yeah, it's me! Come on, let's get you out of here!"

He undid the final knot, and as he did so Julia fell forward into his arms.

Daniel held her tightly, "It's okay," he said. "It's okay, you're safe now."

Daniel took off his jacket and placed it around her, "Here, take this," he said.

He looked into her eyes, "We've got to go!" he said. "Do you understand? We've got to get out of here!"

Julia nodded, her tear-filled eyes gazing into his.

"The fat man's men will be here soon," Daniel said. "I have to find Suzie, but you go, do you understand?"

Julia nodded again.

Daniel handed her the gun, "Here, take this."

"But ..." Julia said, gazing into his eyes. "The ... the files. I ... I have to get the files. They have the names of everyone in the organization."

"Forget the files!" Daniel said. "Just get yourself out! Okay? When Wang's men arrive, this place is going to be like a war zone and you're in no fit shape to do anything. Now, leave! As fast as you can! Got it?"

Julia continued to gaze at him, then she nodded.

Daniel smiled, then leaned forward and kissed her head.

"Take care of yourself," he said, then he turned and limped slightly back towards the door.

Julia followed behind him.

Daniel paused, glancing out into the corridor, then ushered Julia out in front of him and followed her out.

"That way!" he said, pointing for her to go to the right. "I passed a staircase leading up."

"And … and you?" Julia asked, looking at him.

"I have to free some prisoners," Daniel said. "Then find Suzie. You go now! Okay?"

Julia nodded, looking at him one last time.

"Good luck," Daniel said with a smile, then turned and limped along the corridor to the left.

Tears came into Julia's eyes once again as she watched him go.

"Good luck," she said softly, even though Daniel was now too far away to hear her, then she turned and headed along the corridor to the right.

CHAPTER 35

Daniel turned a bend in the corridor and saw the cell doors. He quickly limped towards them taking out the keys that his mother had given him. He was trying the first key in the lock when he heard a noise further along the corridor. He stopped and listened carefully, then he heard footsteps coming towards him, approaching him from around the corridor's bend to the left. Daniel froze, he had no gun. He moved to the side and flattened himself against the wall, deciding to jump out at whoever it was the moment they came into sight. The footsteps came closer, closer …

Daniel squeezed his right hand into a fist and steadied himself on his feet ready to spring out and hit whoever it was.

The footsteps were now louder as they came even closer.

Daniel held his breath.

Suddenly, he saw the man and was about to jump out at him when he stopped himself. His eyes widened and his mouth gaped open when he saw the face of Marshall coming towards him. Marshall saw him and stopped walking.

"M ... Marshall?" Daniel said, an incredulous tone to his voice.

Marshall stared at him in silence, not moving.

"Marshall!" Daniel repeated. "Wha ... what's going on? What ... what are you doing here? You work for them? I can't believe ...!"

Suddenly, a man's voice spoke, but it was not Marshall's.

"McGlade! Hell, you are a wonder! I thought you'd be dead by now!"

The man standing behind Marshall showed himself. Daniel's eyes widened again as he saw Rice. He was standing with a grin on his face holding a gun on Marshall who was standing in front of him.

"Rice?" Daniel said in surprise.

"Daniel," Marshall said, "I ... I didn't know!"

"Shut up!" Rice said, pushing his gun into Marshall's back. "Of course you didn't know!"

Rice glanced at Daniel, "Don't be so surprised McGlade! We knew you'd go to the police. We knew you'd see your friend, so some strings were pulled to get me in on your team to keep tabs on you both. You've got no idea what you've got yourself involved in, have you? People have died for knowing less!"

Daniel made a sudden move but Rice quickly pointed his gun at Marshall's head.

"You make one false move and I'll blow your friend's brain out!" Rice warned.

"Don't worry about me," Marshall said. "They're going to kill us anyway!"

Rice grinned again, "Yeah, that's right. Always playing the hero, right Marshall?"

He looked at Daniel, "Come on! Take a chance! Do you think you can get to me before I put a bullet in his head?"

Daniel hesitated, looking at the gun and then looking at his friend.

"I didn't think so!" Rice said. "Okay, turn around McGlade! I'm putting you both in the cell with the villagers!"

Daniel stared at him bitterly, then looked at Marshall and turned around. Slowly, he walked with his arms raised towards the cell door.

"That's right!" Rice said, pushing Marshall in the back with the gun to move forward. As Daniel reached the cell door, he stopped.

"Open it!" Rice said, taking out a set of keys. He was about to hand Daniel the keys when he noticed the keys already in Daniel's hand. "Well, surprise, surprise! Looks like you've got keys too!" he said, putting his own keys back in his pocket. "Open the door, it's the largest key!"

Daniel chose the largest key and then hesitated, holding it out towards the cell door's lock..

"Open it!" Rice shouted from behind. "And no funny business! My finger's getting itchy on the trigger!"

Slowly, Daniel put the key into the lock, then he turned it and heard a click as the cell door was unlocked.

"Now open the door and get inside!" Rice ordered.

Daniel pushed the door forward. The door creaked slowly open in the following silence. Inside, the cell was dimly lit. Daniel saw that it was a large cell, its rough walls giving it the appearance of a cave. There were people inside, many of them. The people now began to murmur and whisper among themselves as they stared towards Daniel standing in the open doorway. Daniel guessed that there were about a hundred people inside, some of them men and women. Each of them had a worried expression as they stared towards him.

"I said, get inside!" Rice shouted from behind.

"Hey!" Marshall said, before Daniel could move forward.

Daniel turned to look back at him.

"Remember that time down near the beach?" Marshall said.

Daniel stared at him, then shook his head, "No, don't …!" he managed to say, but it was too late.

Marshall threw his head back hitting Rice on the nose behind him and then turned to grapple with the gun in Rice's hand as Rice cried out in pain staggering back a few steps. The gun went off and Marshall cried out clutching at his chest and falling down to the floor. Daniel ran forward towards Rice and before Rice could fire again Daniel reached him and grappled with the gun in Rice's hand. They fell to the floor together, rolling around as they fought, and then another shot rang out and both men stopped moving. Slowly, Daniel pulled himself up and away from Rice staring down at the blood now coming out of Rice's chest. Rice stared back up at him, his eyes glassy. He was dead. Daniel quickly took Rice's gun, then turned and moved over to where Marshall was lying. Blood was coming out of a wound to the right side of his chest. Daniel looked for a pulse, it was faint, but Marshall was still alive. Daniel glanced up and saw the fishing village prisoners moving inside the cell towards the open cell door.

Daniel stared at them for a moment, then shouted up at them, "What are you waiting for?" he shouted. "You're free! Go! Go!"

He wasn't sure if they understood him, but suddenly, they began to run and stumble out of the dimly-lit cell and into the brightly-lit corridor, their eyes squinting in the light. Daniel looked back down at his friend and the pool of blood now covering the floor around him. From the cell behind him, he heard a voice shouting something in Chinese as the people moved quickly forward around him, some of them stumbling over Rice's body as they pushed to get out of the cell. After a moment, Daniel felt a hand on his shoulder and heard a voice speaking to him in English.

"McGlade? …Daniel?"

Daniel glanced up and saw Wang looking down at him.

"Is he …?" Wang started to say, gesturing down towards Marshall.

"He … he's still alive," Daniel managed to say with a choked feeling in his throat, " … barely."

"We have to move fast Daniel!" Wang said, glancing at his watch. "My men should be here soon! We'll come back for him! Did you find out where they're holding my niece?"

Daniel gazed up at him, then looked at the former prisoners now running past him and along the corridor.

"They're angry," Wang said, following Daniel's gaze. "They want to fight."

Daniel shook his head, "They don't stand a chance," he said. "The people here have guns, automatic weapons …"

He glanced up at Wang, "Tell them to stop, tell them to wait for your men!"

"I tried," Wang said, watching the fishing village prisoners run past him. "They won't listen to me." He looked back down at Daniel, "Daniel! … My niece! Where is she?"

Daniel shook his head, looking back down at his friend, "I … I don't know," he said.

"Daniel," Wang said. "We'll come back for him, I promise!"

Daniel continued staring down at his friend, then gave a long sigh, gripped the gun he had taken from Rice in his hand tightly, and looked back up a Wang.

"Okay," he said. "Let's go find her!"

CHAPTER 36

Both Daniel and Wang moved quickly along a passage they'd discovered further along the corridor. The passage had a rough stone staircase leading upwards.

"They put me in the cell with the others," Wang was saying as they ran along the passage. "They thought I was just another fisherman!"

"With a gun and that watch?" Daniel said, glancing back at him as he ran.

"I hid the watch," Wang grinned. "They thought I'd found the gun."

"Count yourself lucky!" Daniel said, now reaching the rough staircase and taking the steps leading up two at a time.

Wang suddenly grabbed Daniel's arm, stopping him. Daniel turned to look back at him.

"Daniel … when you told me about your father … I'm sorry. He was my friend.

Daniel nodded, "I guessed that much. He went to you to help get him out of the country, that's how he met your sister."

Wang nodded, "She helped get him out."

"Makes sense," Daniel said. "So, do I call you uncle or what?"

Wang grinned, "Help me find your sister, and you can call me anything you want!"

Daniel nodded, then turned back and continued on up the staircase. When they reached the top, they stopped. They found themselves on an upper level looking down over the great hall filled with workers busy at the many machines and computers and watched by the guards below.

They both stepped out onto a ledge which wound down towards the hall and saw the catwalks just underneath them. Various armed guards stood on the catwalks surrounding the great hall gazing down at the activity below.

"Any idea how to play this?" Daniel asked, glancing at Wang.

Wang looked at his watch, "I don't understand," he said. "My men should be here by now."

"No offence," Daniel said, looking at him. "But if they're anything like the waiters who work in your restaurant ..."

Suddenly, they heard shots being fired. They looked below and saw a surge of men piling into the great hall and shouting angrily in Chinese as they began to fight with the many workers and guards on the hall floor. Some of the workers fled as the villagers, who had found various objects to use as weapons, ran furiously towards the guards and workers shouting loudly and angrily as they went. The guards fired their weapons hitting some of the villagers running towards them in front, but there were so many angry villagers who had run into the hall that hall's workers and guards were quickly overwhelmed and found themselves being obliged to fight hand to hand.

The guards on the catwalks fired down spraying bullets into the crowd of villagers surging into the hall below them.

"They're going to be slaughtered!" Daniel said, moving to the edge of the ledge. Without a moment's thought he jumped down to the catwalk surprising the guard just below him. Daniel shot the guard before he could turn his weapon on him then picked up the guards machine gun and began firing at the other guards standing on the catwalk around the great hall. He was aware of Wang jumping down onto the catwalk beside him and grabbing another gun from the dead guard at his feet to fire at the other guards who were now crouching down and firing back at them from around the catwalk on which they stood. Suddenly, more shots rang out and more men began running along the catwalk from the other side of the hall firing at the guards. Some of them started climbing down or jumping down into the hall below to help the villagers in their fight against the guards and the workers. Daniel returned machine-gun fire at one of the guards and hit him. The guard cried out and fell back over the rail of the catwalk and down to the hall below. Daniel grinned at Wang who was also firing at another guard.

"Looks like the cavalry's arrived!" Daniel called out above the noise and chatter of machine-gun fire.

"Don't you ever complain about my waiters again!" Wang called back.

Daniel ran along the catwalk still firing and hitting various guards as he went with Wang at his heels. They reached a metal staircase and quickly climbed down it to the hall. When they reached the hall, they began fighting their way through the guards and workers who were fighting against the villagers and Wang's men. The great hall was now in complete chaos. Men were shouting and some of them were crying out and screaming from being beaten or shot.

"This way!" Daniel shouted back to Wang who was hitting a guard just behind him.

Both Daniel and Wang fought their way across the hall to the metal doors leading to the corridor where Daniel had first been taken. One of the workers came at Daniel with a knife as he made for the door and Daniel side-stepped just in time and hit the man across the head with the butt of his machine-gun making him cry out and fall to the floor. Both Daniel and Wang reached the metal doors but found no way to open them. Daniel stepped back, fired the machine-gun towards them, then kicked at the doors, but they still wouldn't open. He turned, crouched down over an unconscious guard lying nearby and checked his pockets. A guard came running towards him with his gun ready to fire but Wang fired first from behind Daniel and the guard cried out and fell back onto the floor. Daniel took out a badge from the unconscious guard's pocket, then stood up and ran back to the large metal doors. He placed the badge up against the side of the doors and then the doors began to slide open. Daniel ran on through into the corridor on the other side followed by Wang, Guards came running towards them from the other end of the corridor firing at them. Both Daniel and Wang crouched firing back at them and   each of guards cried out from the hail of bullets and fell back onto the floor. Daniel ran forward, reached them, and found that one of the guards was still alive. He bent down over the guard and grabbed the lapels of his uniform jacket.

"Where's the girl?" he shouted down at him. "Where's the girl?"

The guard stared up at him saying nothing as blood trickled down from his mouth.

"Let me ask him!" Wang said from behind, moving forward.

Suddenly, Daniel heard a noise and glanced up. He saw man in a white coat who looked like a scientist come out of a room to the left. The scientist saw them and quickly raised his arms staring at the machine gun in Daniel's hands with a fearful expression.

"Don't shoo! Don't shoot!" he cried, now standing still with his arms held high.

Daniel stood staring at him and aiming his machine-gun menacingly towards him.

"Where's the girl?" he shouted, now moving forward and pointing the machine-gun up at the man's face.

The scientist's eyes grew wide, staring at the machine-gun held in front of him. He pointed with a trembling hand back behind him further along the corridor.

"Th … the … the lab!" the man stuttered, staring fearfully at the machine-gun. "The lab!"

Daniel hit the scientist across the head with the butt of the machine-gun. The scientist fell to the floor unconscious, then, followed by Wang, Daniel ran along the corridor towards the other end. Suddenly, as they passed another corridor on the left they saw more guards running towards them.

"Go!" Wang shouted to Daniel as he fired towards the approaching guards. "You go!"

Daniel hesitated looking at him, then turned and continued on along the corridor leaving Wang behind him to take care of the approaching guards.

CHAPTER 37

Heller hesitated for the umpteenth time as he stood over Suzie, placing the blade of the knife down onto the butterfly tattoo.

"Why the hell do you keep on hesitating?" Baines shouted, staring at him. "Go! Go on! Do it!"

Heller sighed, hesitating once again.

"Go ahead!" Baines shouted. "What the hell are you waiting for? You're a butcher aren't you?"

Beneath him, tied to the metal table-top, Suzie lay whimpering and shaking in fear.

Heller looked up back at Baines, "Hey! I'm in the meat business, that's true! But this .... this is a young girl you're talking about!"

Baines grinned, now aiming his gun down towards Heller's stomach, "I don't give a damn if she's a princess! Do it! I'm sure you've done worse in your life!"

"Never to a kid!" Heller said, staring bitterly back into Baines' eyes.

"You've got a choice," Baines said. "It's her … or you!"

Heller glanced back down at Suzie tied helplessly to the table beneath him, hesitating again. Sweat was now trickling down his face. He gripped the knife firmly, then placed it once more down onto the tattoo. He took a deep breath, continuing to hesitate. He felt her body shaking uncontrollably beneath him, then suddenly, with a quick movement, he turned and threw the knife towards Baines. The knife plunged into Baines' stomach before he had time to realize what was happening. He cried out, clutching at his stomach as he stared across at Heller with a look of surprise on his face. Then, before he could fall, Heller leapt forward knocking into him and making him fall to the floor as both men who were standing and watching nearby reached for their guns. Heller grabbed the gun out of Baines' hand and fell to the floor rolling. He quickly fired up at the men. The man to the left cried out falling back but the other man managed to get his gun out and fire down towards Heller. The bullet hit the floor as Heller continued rolling, firing his gun up at him. The second man cried out clutching his chest and then fell back dead before he'd even hit the floor. Heller lay still for a moment looking towards them and breathing a sigh of relief, then slowly, he stood up still holding the gun tightly in his hand as he stared down at the three bodies now lying on the floor around him in a pool of blood. He sighed again, put the gun into his pocket, then turned towards Suzie, the young whimpering Chinese girl bound firmly face down to the metal table. He paused, staring at her for a moment, then he bent down, pulled the knife he'd thrown out of Baines' stomach and then went over to the table.

"Don't worry kid," he said, now cutting the bonds which bound her wrists and ankles to the four corners of the table. "No one's going to hurt you. No one."

When he had finished cutting the bonds, Suzie slowly turned, still whimpering. Her face was bright red with both shame and fear. Tears rolled down her cheeks as she sat up and began to sob and cry, her body shaking in fear. She glanced down at the bodies of the men on the floor, at the pool of blood, strikingly red in contrast to the clinically white floor. Suddenly, bursts of machine-gun fire sounded beyond the closed door. Suzie jumped as she heard them and Heller jerked round to look towards the door.

Heller took the gun back out of his pocket, then turned towards Suzie who sat crying and trembling on the table.

"Don't worry kid," Heller said.

He put an arm around her to comfort her.

"You're safe with me now," he said. "No one's going to harm you."

He looked around and saw another door to the left, then gently pulled Suzie up onto her feet and guided her over towards the door.

"Just stay with me," he said, in a soft reassuring voice. "Everything's going to be fine."

The sound of machine-gun fire from beyond the other door grew louder as Heller glanced round expecting to see guards running into the lab at any second. They reached the other door and Heller quickly pushed Suzie through it and followed her, closing the door behind them. Three dead bodies now lay on the floor of the lab surrounded by pools of blood and an in an eerie silence, save for the sound of the machine-gun fire coming from the corridor outside.

*

The noise of the machine-gun fire from outside the other door grew even louder as it came closer,

and then suddenly, Daniel burst through the door with his machine-gun ready to fire at hip level and into the white room which served as a lab. The first thing he noticed was the blood on the floor, and then as he walked closer, he saw the bodies of the three men. He recognized the thin sadistic looking man called Baines. Daniel moved slowly over to the bodies staring down at them. He glanced at the stainless steel metal table and saw the ropes attached to the four corners which had been cut. He tried to understand what had happened. It was obvious to him that Suzie had been kept there, that she was probably the one who had been tied down to the table. He glanced once again down at the bodies of the men. Someone had helped her. But who? And why? He looked around and noticed the door on the far side of the lab and saw blood-stained footsteps leading over to it. Daniel gritted his teeth and moved quickly across the lab towards the other door, pushing all thoughts about why or who had helped Suzie out of his mind. She was not far now, and he was going to find her. He pushed open the door holding the machine-gun ready for whatever or whoever was beyond it.

CHAPTER 38

The bright-lit corridor twisted and turned leading upwards. Daniel was now running along it. He could hear machine-gun fire somewhere in the distance and from time to time was sure that he could hear someone in the corridor up ahead of him. Suddenly, he rounded a bend and saw them. Heller, with Suzie at his side, were about to enter another corridor leading to the right.

"Hey!" Daniel called out.

Heller spun round at the sound, his gun aimed towards Daniel. Suzie, who was by his side, saw Daniel, her half-brother. Her eyes opened widely and a grin appeared on her face showing her obvious pleasure at seeing him.

"Brother!" she called out, her voice echoing around the walls of the corridor.

"Let her go!" Daniel called out, leveling his machine-gun towards Heller. "Get away from him Suzie!"

Heller stared at the machine-gun then raised his hands defensively as Suzie remained standing beside him.

"Hey, I'm on your side," he said. "They wanted me to butcher this kid with a knife, but I saved her."

"Saved her for yourself?" Daniel asked with a sneer on his face as he moved closer to them.

Suzie suddenly left Heller's side and ran over to Daniel.

"Brother! My brother!" she cried out, as she reached him and hugged him tightly, crying once again.

"She ... she's your sister?" Heller asked in surprised, as he watched the way Suzie was now hugging Daniel.

"Half-sister," Daniel said, eyeing the gun in Heller's hand carefully.

Heller lowered his arms and grinned, "You sure have a way of surprising people!" he said. "Hey, look, I really am on your side! I would never hurt a kid!"

"Drop the gun!" Daniel said to him coldly.

Heller stared at him, then slowly made a move to drop the gun. Suddenly, he went down on one knee and fired. The bullet passed Daniel's head. Daniel struggled to aim the machine-gun towards him but Suzie was still hugging him and restricting his movements. A noise sounded behind him and he jerked his head round just in time to see the guard who'd been sneaking up behind him fall to the floor wide-eyed with a bullet wound in his chest.

"He was about to shoot you in the back!" Heller said.

Daniel stared down at the dead guard, then looked back at Heller.

"Thanks," he said.

"Now do you believe I'm on your side?" Heller asked. "Hell, you saw them shoot my men, right?"

Daniel nodded, gazing at him, then looked down at Suzie. Suzie stared up at him with tear-filled eyes.

"Are you okay?" he asked.

Suzie nodded, "Y ... yes. I ... I'm okay. The man saved me!"

Daniel smiled, then leaned forward, kissed her forehead and hugged her closely.

"Don't worry," he said softly. "I'm here now. I've got you."

"Hey McGlade!" Heller said. "Sorry to break up this family reunion, but we've got to get out of here!"

Daniel glanced across at him, then nodded, "You're right."

He looked down at Suzie, then grabbed her hand, "Stay by me," he said.

"Did you bring the cavalry?" Heller asked, hearing the machine-gun fire in the distance.

Daniel moved forward towards him with Suzie by his side, "You could say that," he said.

"Nice!" Heller said. He looked round at the corridor which led onwards and the corridor branching to the right. "Any idea which way?" he asked.

Daniel shrugged, "Let's try the right," he said.

Suddenly, a noise sounded in the corridor to the right and a giant figure came into view.

"Hugo!" Daniel breathed, staring towards him.

The blonde giant saw them and a sadistic grin came to his face which was still a bloody mess where Daniel had repeatedly hit him in a fit of fury.

"McGlade!" he called out through clenched teeth approaching them along the corridor.

Daniel glanced back at Heller, "Take her!" he said, pushing Suzie towards him.

"Brother! No! Brother!" Suzie cried out as Heller pulled her away from Daniel.

"Take the other corridor!" Daniel said. "Keep her safe!"

Heller glanced at the huge blonde monster advancing along the corridor towards them.

"Right!" he said. "Come on kid!"

He quickly grabbed Suzie's hand and pulled her towards the corridor which led straight on, "This way!" he said.

"No! No! Brother!" Suzie cried out as Heller led her away from Daniel and back towards the other corridor.

Daniel watched them go for a moment, then turned his attention back towards Hugo who was now moving faster along the corridor towards him.

"Oh, the hell with this!" Daniel muttered to himself and aimed the machine-gun towards the approaching giant.

"Say bye-bye," Daniel said, then pressed the trigger.

There was a click, but nothing happened.

"Oh hell," Daniel said to himself, glancing back up towards Hugo. "What a time to run out of bullets."

"McGlade!" Hugo called out once again, his voice loud and filled with anger as he ran towards Daniel as fast as he could, bent on getting his revenge.

CHAPTER 39

Machine-gun fire sounded loudly outside Mr. X's office as the fat man hurriedly went through his desk taking out any important papers that he needed. He stuffed them along with various computer sticks, onto which he'd downloaded important material, into a black bag and zipped it shut. Next, he leaned forward onto his desk to study the computer files. He scrolled down, found the files he was looking for and was about to press delete when the door to his office opened. He glanced up, a worried look on his face, and saw Julia Jones standing there with a gun aimed towards him.

"Get away from the desk!" Julia said coldly.

Mr. X looked at the gun in her hand, and then up at her face. There was no doubt, he was sure, that she would pull the trigger if he didn't comply to the order. He froze, his finger hovering over the delete key.

"I said move away from the computer!" Julia shouted, moving forward further into the office.

A guard suddenly appeared in the open doorway behind her.

"Shoot her!" Mr. X shouted.

But before the guard could do anything, Julia had spun round quickly and shot him. The guard fell back with a cry, hit the corridor wall and slid down to the floor. Mr. X pressed the delete key and grabbed the gun in the open drawer of his desk. As Julia turned back to him, she saw him standing there with a gun in his hand aimed at her stomach. She leapt quickly to the side as he fired two shots. The first shot missed her but the second shot hit her in her left side. Julia cried out falling to the floor and grasping at the bullet wound which seemed to burn her left side in a searing pain. She gasped as blood ran through her fingers to stain the soft white carpeted floor. Mr. X stepped over to her, the gun still in his hand. He looked down at her, his eyes cold, merciless.

"You think you can stop us?" he said bitterly. "We're more powerful than you think! This …" he waved towards the large window which looked out onto the great hall and the people fighting outside, "… this is merely a set-back. And now, Miss Jones," he said through gritted teeth, "say goodbye!"

He pointed his gun down towards her.

Julia glanced at the gun that had dropped from her hand as she fell. It lay just a few feet away. It was close, but too far away for her to reach it.

Suddenly, a villager appeared in the open doorway. Mr. X jerked round as the villager shouted something in Chinese and ran into the office towards him raising a large metal bar he held in his hand ready to strike. The fat man fired quickly hitting the villager and then fired at another villager who appeared behind the first man wielding a knife towards him. The fat man staggered back across his office as he fired at a third, then quickly turned and pressed something in one of the bookcases.

Julia, who had crawled over to reach her gun, now aimed it up towards him. The bookcase moved, sliding to the side to show a secret passage on the other side. Julia fired just as the fat man stepped forward to enter. He cried out in pain, falling against the side of the bookcase, then staggered into the secret passageway and managed to close the bookcase behind him before Julia could fire a second shot. Julia grunted with pain as she pulled herself up onto her knees. She breathed heavily for a moment, gritting her teeth against the pain, then managed to get up onto her feet holding her side. She moved around the desk and slumped down into the chair looking at the computer screen in front of her. She pressed various keys, staining them with the blood from her hand and began trying to recuperate various files. As she was doing so, various screens appeared on the computer showing various parts of the secret underground base. One image interested her in particular. She gasped, gazing at it intensely and seeing Daniel in a corridor called corridor 5 according to the computer. He was about to fight a huge blonde giant who was racing angrily towards him.

*

Hugo threw his gun down to one side as he ran, then hit Daniel with a force that knocked him down to the floor. Hugo fell on top of him reaching for Daniel's throat. Daniel grunted and strained, holding Hugo's wrists, trying to keep those huge hands away from him. Suddenly, he jerked his head forward and hit Hugo on his broken nose. Hugo yelled out in pain and Daniel was able to push him to one side and roll away from under him. Daniel got to his feet staring across at Hugo, his fists ready, as Hugo stared back at him, getting slowly up onto his feet.

"I was going to rip your throat out with my bare hands!" Hugo said through gritted teeth.

He glanced at Daniel's fists with a worried expression, remembering the beating they'd given him, then he looked down towards the gun he had thrown to the floor. He bent forward and reached for the gun staring at Daniel all the while. "But I guess a bullet in the gut will be just as good," he said.

He grinned a vicious grin as he stood back up with the gun in his hand staring across at Daniel as he aimed the gun towards Daniel's gut.

"No!"

The scream had come from a woman's voice. There was a quick movement, then the woman appeared from a bend in the corridor to the left running towards Hugo and jumping up against him. Hugo jerked round towards her and then a shot sounded as he fired the gun just as the woman hit him knocking him back off balance. The woman screamed, crying out in pain and doubled over clutching at her stomach, then she staggered, falling forward against Hugo's body, who had now regained his balance. Slowly, she slid down against him to slump to the floor at his feet.

Daniel remained frozen to the spot as he stared down at the woman who had saved him, recognizing the woman as Miss Clarke, his mother. He trembled as he stared down at her body.

"M ... mother!" he cried out.

For a moment, Hugo didn't move. He stood staring down in surprise at the woman who had taken the bullet that was meant for Daniel, then slowly, he glanced back up at Daniel, and with an expression of anger and pure hatred on his face, he raised the gun up towards him again. His eyes stared coldly across at Daniel as his finger began to pull on the gun's trigger. Suddenly, another shot rang out from a different gun. Hugo stared wide-eyed, then glanced down at the blood stain now growing across his chest. Another shot rang out, then another, each of them hitting Hugo in the chest. Hugo's gun clattered to the floor, he teetered on his feet, then he fell down to the floor dead.

Daniel ran across to his mother crying and shouting.

"Mother! Mother!" he shouted, now grabbing her body and picking her up to him so that he could hold her tightly in his arms.

"Mother!" he shouted again, as he cried against her. "Mother!"

Felicity appeared from around the corridor corner staring down at Daniel in both shock and surprise, observing the way he called Miss Clarke mother and grasped her in his arms, holding her tightly against him. After a moment, Daniel glanced up and saw Felicity standing just a few feet from him holding the gun she'd shot Hugo with.

"You … you call her mother?" Felicity said, a tone of shock and surprise in her voice.

Daniel nodded, he gazed back down at his mother's body, and then gently laid her back down onto the floor. He stared down at her for a moment, then stood up. Felicity raised the gun, aiming it towards him as he did so.

"She … she was my mother," Daniel said, now looking into Felicity's eyes.

Felicity stared back at him, then shook her head.

"No ... no! That ... that's not possible!"

Daniel could see the tears in Felicity's eyes.

He took a step towards her but Felicity moved back holding the gun tightly in her hand as she continued to aim it towards him.

"Look at me Felicity," Daniel said. "Look past the bruises and the cuts, but ... look at me! Don't you feel it? I felt it the first moment I saw you! I didn't understand it then, but I understand it now. We're twins Felicity. Twins! You ... and me, we ... we're twins! Your ... 'our' mother sacrificed herself for me. She saved my life! Do you think she would do that if ... if I wasn't her son?"

Tears began to fall onto Felicity's cheeks as she continued to aim her gun towards him.

"No!" she said, shaking her head. "No! My mother's dead! And it's because of you! Because of you!"

Daniel reached out his hand.

"Felicity ... give me the gun. You're sick Felicity, let me ... let me help you. I can help you ... please."

Felicity continued shaking her head as she wiped away her tears with one hand..

"You ... you feel it, don't you?" Daniel asked softly. "You feel there's something between us."

"No!"

Felicity's hands now began shaking as she continued aiming the gun towards him.

"Okay then …" Daniel said, holding out his arms,

"… shoot me. Shoot your brother Felicity. Shoot your twin brother, … go ahead!"

Felicity sobbed, her hands continuing to shake. She continued to aim the gun at him, her finger on the trigger, then suddenly she sobbed, and then she began to lower the gun aimed at him.

"Felicity!" a voice shouted loudly along the corridor.

Daniel turned and saw Julia staggering along the corridor towards them, blood coming from a wound in her side, her right hand raised and aiming a gun directly towards Felicity as she stared at the younger punk-looking girl with eyes full of hate.

"No!" Daniel shouted.

He leapt forward towards his sister just as Julia pulled the trigger. The shot sounded echoing in the corridor just a Daniel managed to knock his sister out of the way. The bullet ripped into him, forcing a cry from him as he fell back from its force onto the floor and rolled. Felicity stood frozen, staring down at the blood starting to appear in her brother's chest. She looked round at Julia who had now fallen to her knees and was staring at Daniel's body in wide-eyed shock.

"Nooo!" Julia screamed.

Daniel's eyes were still open. He tried to say something up to Felicity, his twin sister, as she stared down at him, but the words would not come, and then suddenly, she was not there, she had gone, and then a darkness surrounded him and a black veil of unconsciousness draped itself down over him.

CHAPTER 40

Daniel slowly opened his eyes and winced in the bright sunlight streaming in through the window to his right. He turned his head and saw white-laced curtains billowing back into the room from the breeze coming through the open window. Outside, the sky was blue, a beautiful blue.

"Brother?"

Daniel turned his head and saw Suzie sitting by his bedside. She leaned forward, gazing down into his eyes, then reached for his hand and grasped it tightly in hers.

"My brother … Daniel … you … you're going to be all right!"

He noticed the tears in her eyes and how she almost choked on the words as she spoke.

She smiled down at him, then stood up, "I … I'll get you the doctor, tell him you're awake!"

She turned and quickly left the room before Daniel could say anything.

A few moments later, the door to his room opened, but it wasn't the doctor who walked in. Daniel glanced up at his visitor in surprise. The Chief closed the door behind him and walked over to the bed.

"How are you feeling?" the Chief asked.

"Wha … what are you doing here?" Daniel asked, looking up at him in surprise.

The Chief reached into his pocket and took out a gun, "Marshall's barely hanging in," he said. "You and Marshall, you've been causing all kinds of problems. When I finish with you, he's next."

He pulled out a silencer from another pocket. Daniel stared in shock as the Chief began to fix the silencer onto the gun.

"It … it was you!" Daniel said. "You! You're the one who framed me! You've been working for …!"

"Spider," the Chief said, finishing Daniel's sentence for him. "That's right. I got Rice in to keep an eye on you and Marshall. We knew you had the girl. Imagine our surprise when we learned that you couldn't remember anything! They must have really whacked you on the head too hard. We knew that your father still had a friend in the organization, a John Keaton. You met him. Your father sent you the girl, and her mother too, but you were able to hide the girl and the mother away before we found out about it. Your father contacted Keaton to help you. We tortured him for nothing, he had no idea where you'd hid them." The Chief sighed, "You know, Mr. X is very upset about what has happened. Now, I have orders to kill you." He shrugged, "It grieves me, but there it is."

"Why?" Daniel asked. "Why would you ...?"

"Work for Spider?" The Chief said.

He grinned, "If you knew how much they offered me, you wouldn't be asking. Some of the people involved are millionaires, you know that?"

He raised the gun and aimed it down at Daniel's head.

"Waiting for your sister to come back with the doctor are you?" the Chief said. "Tsk, tsk ... I'm afraid something may have happened to your sister on the way to him."

"You!" Daniel said bitterly, trying to get up.

"Goodbye McGlade!"

Suddenly, the door burst open and a shot was fired. The Chief seemed to freeze, his eyes widening wildly. The gun he held fell out of his hand and clattered to the floor, and then he fell forward and down to the floor beside the bed.

Daniel breathed a sigh of relief and then looked up towards the door. The door opened wider and Daniel saw Heller standing there with a gun in his hand.

He grinned down at Daniel.

"You know, I've always wanted to plug a Chief of police!" he said.

Suzie ran into the room from behind him.

"Brother! Brother! Are you all right?" she shouted, running to his bed-side and leaning forward to place her arms around him.

"We got the other guy," Heller said, nodding towards another man who was being pushed into the room by the tall man who worked for Heller.

Daniel gasped in surprise as he stared up at Sergeant Greene, the desk Sergeant at the police station.

"They were going to take care of your sister," Heller said. "But we took care of them instead!"

Daniel noticed the bump on the Greene's head and the way his wrists were handcuffed behind his back.

"Thanks," Daniel said. "Again!"

Heller grinned down at him, "You're welcome. I wouldn't let anybody hurt the kid!"

Daniel nodded understandingly with a smile, looking at Heller as if he were truly seeing at him for the first time. He glanced down at his sister who was still hugging him tightly, then leaned forward and gently kissed her on the head. The fact that she was only his half sister and half Chinese didn't matter to him at all. No, the halves didn't matter. In fact, as far as Daniel was concerned, there were no halves, no borders, only feelings, really, really true feelings.

CHAPTER 41

Three months later.

The surf rolled in gently up onto the beach. Daniel sat on the sand gazing up at the beautiful pastel colours of the sky as a golden sun began to set. This was his favourite time of the day, and being near the ocean was his favourite place.

"Thought I'd find you here," said a voice as someone walked up to him from behind and sat down next to him.

Daniel looked at Julia and smiled.

"How's the side?" he asked.

Julia shrugged, "It's okay. I just have to be careful not to laugh too much for a few more months. You?"

"Oh, you know me, a black cat, always bouncing back up."

Julia returned his smile.

"How's Suzie?" she asked.

"She's okay. She's with Jack right now."

"Heller?" Julia asked in a surprised tone of voice.

Daniel nodded, "She calls him 'uncle'. They get on well together. He's like a big kid around her. He treats her like his niece. I guess he missed not having kids."

"So, she's got two uncles now," Julia said.

"Yeah," Daniel said, "Wang's the other one. She's certainly got a strange family!"

Julia smiled, "You know, technically, Wang's your uncle too, right?"

Daniel grinned, "Technically," he said. "Just don't remind me, that's all."

Julia laughed, then winced from the pain in her side.

"Sorry,' Daniel said, looking at her.

"It's okay. You know, since we had the micro-chip surgically removed leaving no scars, Suzie's not in danger anymore.'

"Yeah, well, Jack wants to take precautions, and as her brother, so do I."

Julia nodded, "I understand." She glanced towards the sunset. The sky was a mixture of pink, red and purple as the sun began to set on the horizon.

"You know, things are coming back to me now," Daniel said. "Keaton, he told me about Spider. I didn't know what to believe at the time, it … it was all too much for me, a shock. He took me to the warehouse which he said was being used by the organization, he wanted to prove to me that everything was true."

"And that's when you got caught," Julia said. "Spider moved out just after, leaving behind an empty warehouse." Julia said.

She sighed glancing down, "I'd never seen anybody tortured before. You know, I've left the agency."

Daniel looked at her.

"Really? Why? You're a good agent."

Julia shrugged, "Oh, they wanted me to stay. I managed to retrieve some important information from Mr. X's computer before the files were completely deleted."

"Did you find the mole in your organization?" Daniel asked.

Julia nodded, "Yes, we got him. Apparently, he was putting out a contract to kill you, you were too close, you knew too much."

"It's great to be liked!" Daniel said. "So … now you're a kind of hero."

Julia glanced down pensively, then shook her head.

"That's not the way I see it," she said. "Your … your twin sister, Felicity, … she … she did things to me that … that I can never forget. She … she broke me. I … I told her everything … everything!"

A sob seemed to catch in her throat

Daniel mover closer to her and placed his arm around her.

"Anybody would have broken under ..."

"No! No! It ... it happened to me! And ... and I thought I was strong! I thought I could resist! I mean ... a good agent is supposed to resist, right?"

"Julia," Daniel said, squeezing her gently. "It's not your fault. You were tortured."

Julia shrugged, "Anyway ... I ... I decided to leave the agency."

Daniel studied her.

"What are you going to do now?" he asked.

Julia shrugged again, "I don't know. Wang, your uncle, ... he's offered me a job ... office work for his agency ... not in the field. I'm considering it."

Daniel smiled, "Okay," he said. "Maybe office work instead of field work would suit you. I just want to say that ... well ... I owe you my life Julia. I'll never forget that."

Julia turned and gazed into Daniel's eyes. In the fading light of the sunset, Daniel saw the tears in her eyes.

She touched his cheek gently, then leaned forward and kissed him lightly on the lips.

"Thank you," she said softly.

Daniel smiled, but remained still.

Julia continued to gaze into his eyes, waiting, thinking that he would kiss her, but he didn't.

After a moment, Julia turned and glanced down, disappointed that he'd made no move towards her.

"Well ... I ... I guess I should go,' she said, getting to her feet. "I just ... I just came by to see how you were."

Daniel stood up with her.

"Thanks,' he said.

Julia looked at him, her eyes gazing into his as if she were searching, searching to see what was behind them.

"Well ... goodbye Daniel!" she said suddenly, then abruptly turned and walked back across the beach towards her car parked in the road.

Daniel stood watching as she got into her car and started the engine. Julia turned back to look at him one last time, then she drove her car forward along the road which ran parallel to the beach. Daniel remained still, watching the red tail-lights of her car disappear into the darkness which was now beginning to settle on the city, then he sat back down on the beach and once again looked towards the horizon and the fading colours of the sky.

*

A shadow lurked beside one of the buildings which looked onto the beach. The person remained still, observing Daniel as he sat alone on the beach thinking. Apart from Daniel, and one man walking his dog, the beach was completely empty. A car came along the beach road moving slowly and approaching the part of the beach where Daniel was sitting. The person in the shadows watched as the car stopped and two men got out. The men spoke quietly together for a moment, then they stepped off the road and began to walk across the beach towards Daniel.

Daniel heard the footsteps on the sand behind him and turned to look round. He saw the two men. Both were heavy set and wearing smart suits, each of them with a white shirt and tie. Apart from the guns with the silencers attached to them which they held in their hands, the men looked like normal business men. Daniel saw the guns and moved fast to take out his own gun.

"Tsk, tsk! Not a good idea!' the man on the right said, wagging his finger from side to side and down at Daniel as if Daniel were merely a schoolboy.

Daniel stared up at the two guns aimed down towards him with the silencers and froze.

"Take out your gun slowly," the other man said. "Finger-tips on the handle only. That's right, now, throw it to the right."

Daniel complied, throwing his gun a few feet away to the right.

"What is this?" Daniel asked, staring up at them both.

The man who'd wagged his finger at him grinned.

"Compliments of Mr. X," he said.

Both men raised their guns and aimed them down towards Daniel's chest.

Suddenly, two shots rang out.

Both men cried out. The man on the left fell down to his knees, while the man on the right fell forward head-first into the sand. The man on the left stared wide-eyed at Daniel for an instant, then tried to raise his gun towards him. Another shot rang out and the man fell forward onto the sand dead. Daniel stared down at the two bodies, then looked up. Across the beach, just nearby the road, he managed to see a girl. She was lowering the gun she held in both hands.

"Felicity!" Daniel said softly to himself in surprise, recognizing his twin sister.

Daniel quickly retrieved his gun, got to his feet, and then ran across the beach towards her.

"Felicity!" he called out. "Felicity!"

But by the time he'd reached the road, she was gone.

*

A full moon hung in the sky casting a silvery light down onto the deserted city streets below. It was late, and the city was sleeping. A long shadow moved along one dimly-lit street from beneath the yellow light of an overhead streetlamp. It moved alone and in silence. After a moment, the shadow stopped moving. Felicity stood in the centre of the road gazing up at the full moon. There were tears in her eyes. She glanced at the windows of the surrounding buildings thinking of the people sleeping soundly and safely behind them, then she moved forward once more, like a lone shadow, disappearing into the darkness of the night.

The end.

ABOUT THE AUTHOR

Lawrence Nabbs (Larry) was born in London, England. He wrote his first short story at the age of eleven. He later started to write poems and other short stories. He was given the idea for his first novel length story after having had the strange experience of seeing UFOs in France. Since then, Larry has enjoyed writing novel length stories, but still writes poems from time to time. In England, he did different jobs, not really finding himself until he went to Paris, France, to become an English teacher where he lived and worked as a teacher for over twenty years, therefore he also speaks French. He later went to Beijing, China, in the year 2006 where he continues to teach English and write novel length stories, such as crime thrillers, science fiction and fantasies. He has also written stories for a children's comic in China for learning English. He loves the cinema, films of all kinds, as well as books and music. He likes and very often writes stories in cafes, and also loves the feeling of being near the ocean.

www.ingramcontent.com/pod-product-compliance
Lightning Source LLC
Chambersburg PA
CBHW020242180626
46810CB00006B/2323